Rose's Story

Rose's Story

A PREQUEL TO THE STRUNG TRILOGY

PER JACOBSEN

HUMBLEBOOKS

Rose's story

Cover art: Per Jacobsen

ISBN (paperback): 978-87-94319-28-7
ISBN (hardback): 978-87-94319-27-0

To my wonderful, loyal readers.
Many of you have expressed the same wish;
that I write more books in the STRUNG universe.
This one is for you.

Other books by Per Jacobsen

The Mansion of Mirrors (2020)

Strung (2021)

Strung II: The Valley of Death (2022)

Strung III: The Last Drop (2022)

The Rude Awakening of Theodor Moody (2023)

Dry (2023)

Do we know each other? If we do, there's a reasonable chance we've met via the *Strung* trilogy, and maybe that's precisely why you're holding this book in your hands. If so, all is well, and I wish you a good read.

If, on the other hand, we don't know each other, I feel I should tell you that although *Rose's Story* chronologically is a prequel to the *Strung* series, it was written *after*. And if you want to get the most out of *Rose's Story*, that is probably also how it should be read; *after Strung 1, 2,* and *3*.

In the end, of course, it's entirely up to you. In any case, I am just happy and grateful that you have decided to spend some of your precious time reading my words.

—PER JACOBSEN

PART ONE

The Gym

"Roses are red, violets are blue.
Flashing those colors, they're coming for you."

O. E. Geralt

Chapter One

The sound of the door handle being pushed down, followed by the creaking of the hinges, along with the muffled sound of footsteps on a carpet.

It's these three sounds that wake Rose Lavine this morning, and it's only later—several *days* later—she realizes that this was the first sign of something being very wrong with her mom.

Because despite the many changes their home has seen since Rose's father crashed his truck and died five years ago, one thing has never changed.

The morning routine. It's a ritual in three steps. It starts with nine knocks on the door to Rose's room to the bass rhythm from Queen's hit *Another One Bites the Dust*. Then the same knocking rhythm is repeated, this time on the door to Sebastian's room. The last step is the sound of their mom's melodic voice announcing that their breakfast is ready.

Today, however, there are no knocks on the door, and her mom's voice isn't melodic. It's flat, almost robotic, as she says:

"Good morning, Rose. It's time to get up. You don't want to miss the bus."

Rose lifts her head from the pillow and stares at her through a hazy veil of sleepiness and confusion, but she doesn't have time to say anything before her mom has disappeared out the doorway again. A second later, she hears the door to Sebastian's room open. He gets the same toneless wake-up call, and then their mom heads down the stairs to the ground floor.

For a moment, Rose considers calling her back to ask if she's okay, but a loud clunk from inside Sebastian's room pushes the thought aside.

"What are you doing?"

"Nothing," Sebastian drones in a *mind your own business* tone. After a short pause, however, he adds, with a somewhat gentler timbre: "I stepped on the cord to my phone, so it fell on the floor. Crap."

Rose smiles and shakes her head, then pushes herself up from the bed and walks over to her wardrobe. Through the years, many different faces have adorned the closet door, but the current resident, a smiling Ed Sheeran, has been allowed to stay for an extra long time. That's the least Rose can do for the man who made it cool to be a redhead like her.

After pulling on a pair of jeans and a loose-fitting sweater, she leaves her room and goes out into the hallway. Her destination is the bathroom, but she only manages to take a few steps toward it before Sebastian comes flying out the door to his room and scrambles past her.

"Me first!"

"Seriously, Sebastian? Stop being such a—"

Slam! Click! The bathroom door is shut and locked. She lost the battle even before it started.

"At least give me my toothbrush."

A long pause while he considers. Then the door is opened, and his hand shoots out, delivers the toothbrush, and disappears again.

Irritated—and frankly amazed that Sebastian is still so immature, even though he turned twelve this summer—Rose stomps down the stairs to the ground floor. At least they have two bathrooms in the house. Otherwise, she would probably have strangled him a long time ago.

When she's done brushing her teeth, Rose borrows her mom's hairbrush and sorts out the most disobedient locks of her red hair. She could also borrow some makeup from the bag in the drawer, but after a sample smile to her reflection in the mirror, she decides to skip that today. Undoubtedly, her skin will appreciate it. So will her stomach, which is more than ready to get some breakfast ... and lets her know with an impatient growl.

"Smells good," she says as she steps into the kitchen.

Evidently, her mom has been absorbed in her own thoughts, because she jolts and almost drops the spatula in her hand.

"It's pancakes," she replies, gesturing toward the counter, where there is a plate with a small tower of pancakes next to a bottle of maple syrup.

"Um, yeah. I ... see that. Looks delicious."

The morning meal *is* delicious, but also rather unexpected, since this is a completely ordinary Wednesday. Usually, pancakes are reserved for week-ends and holidays. On top of that, there's still some-thing about her mom's voice that feels wrong. Rose can't quite put her finger on it, but she sounds so ...

Absent?

Yeah, that's a fair word to describe it. She sounds absent—as if she were a robot just reciting some dry fact. *Water is wet, deserts are hot, and this is a plate full of pancakes.*

"Oh, nice!" sounds behind her as Sebastian enters the kitchen and spots the feast.

"Yes, isn't it?" Betty Lavine replies in her robotic

voice ... but, of course, it goes over Sebastian's head that his mom sounds as if the will to live has just seeped out of her. He has eyes for nothing but the pancakes, which he grabs one of in passing and devours while pouring a glass of juice—and as soon as that's down, he grabs the plate with the entire stack and brings it with him to the dining table in the center of the kitchen.

"You'd better hurry up if you also want some," her robot mom says, smiling at Rose. A smile that also seems put-on.

"What? Uh, yeah, sure," Rose replies, taking a seat at the table.

Whatever is weighing down her mom hasn't affected her ability to make pancakes. Rose concludes this at the very first bite—and after the third or fourth mouthful, she has almost forgotten her worries about her mom's strange behavior.

However, they return, even stronger, soon after. The reason is her mom's reaction to what is happening outside the kitchen window. Or rather; her *lack* of reaction to it.

Their house is an old two-story brick house located in a small neighborhood in Coulton, and from the kitchen window all three of them have a view of the road as well as a good portion of the houses over on the other side.

They also have a view of their own driveway and front yard. The latter is the life and passion of Betty Lavine. She has what you'd call *a green thumb*, and hardly a day passes without her bringing out the garden shears to trim and adjust something.

For the same reason, she isn't pleased if passers-by step a little too far outside the pavement tiles and leave footprints in her flower beds.

And she *really* isn't pleased if someone lets their doggies stomp around in there.

Old Harold McGee from down in number 27 does exactly that. He takes three daily walks with Frankie; a gray-bearded French Bulldog who is just as grumpy as Harold himself. Each one of these three walks takes them past the front yard of the Lavine house ... and, in Frankie's case, often well into it.

That, in itself, is enough to send Rose's mom up in the red zone. But sometimes it doesn't stop there. Sometimes Frankie leaves a gift for her, in the middle of the flowerbed, and Harold ... well, let's just say he's not the type of dog owner who likes to carry a roll of bags in his pocket.

Nothing in the whole wide world can get Betty Lavine's blood boiling faster than the sight of Frankie squatting between her petunias.

Under normal circumstances.

Today, however, she is completely unaffected when

Harold and Frankie appear on the sidewalk. She also doesn't react when Harold stops and gives the chubby little bulldog free rein to stomp on her flowers.

And she neither grimaces nor winces when the animal drops a huge, steaming pile of shit in the middle of the bed and then trudges on down the street with its owner.

She didn't see it, Rose thinks. *She must have been focusing on something across the road, so she didn't see them at all.*

Except that she would have to be completely blind not to have seen it. She stood right in front of the kitchen window, and her eyes followed them from start to finish.

Rose glances at her little brother, who is holding a half-eaten, rolled up pancake still in the air in front of his mouth, looking as shocked and confused as she feels.

What the hell? he mimes.

I don't know, Rose mimes back, shrugging.

"Uh, Mom?"

"Yes, Rose?"

"Are you, um ... are you okay?"

"I'm fine. Why?"

Monotonous voice, expressionless eyes, and a smile so phony that it makes Rose cringe and lose her voice.

"It's just ... Frankie was out in the flowers again," Sebastian says, coming to her rescue. "You usually get pretty mad about that."

Under her light brown bangs, their mom squints her eyes as if wondering if that really is true. Then she shrugs her shoulders.

"Mr. McGee probably just forgot to bring bags," she says, after which she bends down and opens the cupboard under the sink. "I'll get it. I was on my way out with the garbage anyway."

As if to show that these aren't just empty words, she pulls out the garbage bag, ties a knot on it, and holds it up for them to see. Then she turns around and strolls out of the kitchen with it in hand.

Rose exchanges another glance with Sebastian, who opens his eyes wide and shakes his head as he shoves the last mouthful of his fourth or fifth pancake into his mouth.

"You'll need a warm jacket today," their mom says when she returns to the kitchen a minute later. "Fall is here. And bring an umbrella too. It feels like it's gonna rain today."

Again, the words are fine, but her toneless delivery of them ...

"Anything exciting happening at school today?" she continues, directing her blank gaze at Rose.

"Well, exciting is a strong word," Rose replies, "but

that police thing is today, so we don't have math in first period."

"Oh yeah, I completely forgot that was today," her robot mom says without a trace of real interest, before letting her gaze slide down to her wristwatch. "Then you'd better finish up and get going so you won't be late."

After breakfast, Rose and Sebastian put on their jackets and get ready in the hallway. That's another fixed ritual that has been strictly enforced since their dad died. Every morning, their mom puts a hand on their shoulders, looks them in the eye, and tells them to take care of themselves and each other.

Today, she stays in the kitchen.

"Uh, Mom?"

"Yes, hon?"

"Aren't you going to say goodbye?"

A pause. Then a clinking sound, followed by quick footsteps, and their mom appears in the doorway, lips curled up in a stiff smile.

"Sorry," she says, raising her hand for a wave. "Have a good day at school, okay? I'll see you this afternoon."

"Um ... thanks, Mom," Rose manages to stutter, before she—hesitantly and a little perplexed—turns around and walks out the front door with Sebastian.

The nearest bus stop is some distance away, and

the walk there feels eerily identical every day—verging on déjà vu. The reasons are simple enough, though. One is that in a neighborhood like this, there is an unwritten rule that everyone keeps their houses and lawns to a certain standard, and this means that major changes are rarely made. The second reason is that it's the same people they meet—and the same conversations they have—every single day.

The first encounter is Mrs. Thompson, who always sits on her white porch with her morning coffee, waving as they pass by. Two houses further on, Wilma Bishop awaits. Literally, that must be what Wilma does, because otherwise it's a pretty freaky coincidence that she always happens to be taking out the trash at the exact moment they pass her driveway. Even on the few days when they've overslept and left home later it has held true.

And Mrs. Bishop always greets them with the same words. She also does today, even though she sounds a bit more tired than usual.

"Time for school again, huh?"

"Good morning, Mrs. Bishop. Yeah, it is, unfortunately."

"You should be happy about it. I wish I'd had the same opportunities when I was your age. But it was a different time back then."

"It sure was, Mrs. Bishop. Well, we'd better get a move on so we don't miss the bus."

"Yes, of course. Tell your mom I said hi, okay?"

"We will."

The final daily greeting is the only one that Rose actually looks forward to. That's when they pass the fenced playground outside Coulton's only daycare center, the House of the Bumblebees. Here, one or two adults usually sit on a blanket with a group of small children—and they always pause what they are doing to wave and shout good morning in chorus.

Chapter Two

Half an hour later, Rose sits on a bus seat, staring at the landscape sliding by behind her reflection in the window. Her mom was right; fall has come to Coulton. The leaves on the trees have changed to an unobtrusive color scheme of orange and brown shades, and even here, behind the glass of the window, she can sense how cold the wind is out there.

A faint pulling sensation in her body, followed by the sound of a hydraulic brake, tells her that the bus has reached its next stop, Pine Hill Middle School, which means two things: Her pancake-obsessed little brother is getting off, and her cute guy-obsessed friend is getting on.

"See you later, Sis," Sebastian mutters, patting the headrest of her seat as he passes her on the way out.

Rose responds with a half-hearted groaning sound. That's the most he'll get after the bathroom stunt this morning.

Truth be told, she isn't really angry about it. Part of her is glad that he is still so childish. Because who knows what he's going to be like once the puberty train hits him. She has seen several of the boys in her class go from being fun and sociable to being timid and voiceless. Some of her former best friends can hardly even look her in the eye while talking to her. And looking at it that way, she'd still prefer an infantile prankster of a little brother to a moody pessimist isolating himself in his room.

"Hey, Red. Ready to drool over hot guys in uniforms?"

"Hey, Kitty," Rose replies, rolling her eyes in response to the question.

"What?" Kitty laughs as she crams her bag in under the seat in front of them and then takes a seat next to Rose. "You're going to tell me you don't think police uniforms are *hot*?"

Following the last word, she shakes her hand and blows on it as if she has just touched something burning hot. And, typically Kitty, she makes sure that the three boys in the back seat of the bus also catch the show.

Kitty's real name is Katherine, but she has hated

that name for as long as Rose has known her, and after several attempts—*Kate, Katie, Kat, Kay, etc.*—Kitty ended up being the nickname that caught on. Perhaps due to the fact that even after switching to high school, she carried her books in a pink *Hello Kitty* bag. Also typical her.

"Uniforms *can* be hot," Rose admits. "But when it's on old Hodge ... not so much."

Hodge is Ben Hodge. He's the sheriff of Coulton county, and he's had that job all of Rose's life. And probably her mom's whole life too.

"Christ, not Hodge," Kitty says, wrinkling her tiny snub-nose. "His assistant, the new guy. I'd gladly let him put me in handcuffs."

Once more, Rose's eyes roll upward.

"And what about Mark? You think he'll like that idea?"

Kitty responds by waving her hand as if to say there's no need to get hung up on trivial details, but then her eyes widen.

"Oh yeah! I almost forgot that I wanted to tell you. Mark was really strange yesterday."

"How?"

"He was like ... weird. As if he didn't want to be at my house at all."

"Was he mad about something?"

Kitty stares thoughtfully into the air for a moment. Then she shakes her head.

"No, not mad. Just … indifferent." She lowers her voice to a whisper and leans over toward Rose. "He didn't even want to fool around. And Mark *always* wants to fool around."

"Oh, yeah, that does sound strange," Rose says. She tries to appear genuinely interested, but it's not always easy to take the problems in Kitty and Mark's relationship seriously. Because they are both very … *dramatic* is probably a fitting word, and their issues are rarely as gigantic as her friend makes them out to be.

She waits a moment to see if Kitty intends to continue the conversation. Since that doesn't seem to be the case, she turns her face back to the bus window and the bleak autumn landscape outside.

It's raining now. Of course. And she can't even say that she wasn't warned, because her mom suggested that they bring an umbrella … which neither Rose nor Sebastian did.

"My mom was pretty weird this morning too," she murmurs, in part to Kitty and in part as a thought she says out loud to her own reflection in the rain-soaked window.

"Yeah?" Kitty replies with about the same interest that the average citizen shows the homeless person on the street holding a *The apocalypse is near, find Jesus before it's too late* cardboard sign.

"She, um ... she made pancakes."

A pause. Then Kitty smacks both hands down on her thighs.

"You're kidding! Pancakes? Did you call social services?"

"Oh come on, Kitty. It's just weird with the pancakes because it's a school day, but it was more than that. She was ... absent. Like totally off."

"You mean indifferent? Like Mark?"

Rose shrugs.

"Maybe, I ... no, I don't know. She just wasn't herself, that's all."

Halfway expecting to be getting another smart comment, she meets her friend's gaze.

Kitty surprises her. She doesn't have a playful smile on her lips, and she doesn't make fun of her. Instead, she gently pushes her arm with her elbow.

"Your mom is just having a bad day. We've all got them."

"Yeah, I guess," Rose mutters, returning her gaze to the window just in time to see the town sign glide by as they leave Coulton.

Fifteen minutes later, the bus stops in front of Oakwood High School and the two friends get out, after which they sprint across the large common area to get shelter from the rain. However, halfway up the stairs leading to the entrance hall, Rose is struck by a realization that causes her to slow down and then stop completely.

With the exception of herself, Kitty, and a boy in a dark blue hoodie with the text *I PAUSED MY GAME TO BE HERE* written across its chest, none of the students from the bus are running. They stroll along, carefree as ever, with their bags hanging on shoulders that gradually get more and more soaked by the icy raindrops. And they are completely indifferent. What the heck is wrong with—

"Hey, Red! You coming?"

"Huh? Yeah, sorry, Kitty. I'm on my way."

Chapter Three

As always at this time of morning, the entrance hall at Oakwood High is a busy place. Students and teachers buzz around like bees in a flowery meadow. If it weren't for the colorful posters adorning the walls, showcasing the school's athletic competitions, drama shows, scholarly accomplishments, and club events, the place could easily be mistaken for the hub of a train station.

But it's not just the bustling atmosphere that contributes to that impression. The architecture of the large room—the tall, curved ceiling structures and the marble floor, polished to perfection—are also reminiscent of large train stations.

Today, however, Rose notices neither the floor nor the ceiling in the entrance hall. Her eyes are fixed on something else. They are locked on the three young boys who are talking to each other next to the door to the toilets.

"This day just keeps getting weirder," whispers Kitty, who has also spotted them now.

Rose nods but says nothing. She just continues to stare, trying to figure out if her eyes are somehow deceiving her.

The boys are Dean Husky, Roy Parker, and Albert Short. They stand in a small semicircle, talking about something on the pages of the binder Albert holds in his hands.

Presumably it's homework—*biology*, if one were to guess from the title on the cover of the binder—and for an external observer, there would be nothing wrong with the sight of three boys doing a last-minute study of a lesson before the start of class.

But it *is* wrong. Very, very wrong.

First of all, Rose is pretty sure that Dean and Roy aren't in the habit of wasting their time on homework when there are more important things—such as cheerleaders and football—to worry about. Secondly, their normal reaction at the sight of Albert with a binder would have been to call him something nasty and then follow up by knocking the binder out of his hands.

Today, the nerd and the two bullies stand side by side, and they talk to each other, calmly and politely, in turn pointing down at the papers of the binder. As if they are working together, trying to solve a challenging academic problem. It makes no—

A sharp, metallic ring from the wall behind her causes Rose to jolt. It's the school bell, informing the students that the first class is about to start.

She exchanges a glance with Kitty, who was obviously also startled by the sound, and then they both let out a spontaneous, chuckling laughter.

"I think we should have just stayed home today, Red," Kitty says as they start to walk down the hall toward the classroom.

Rose smiles and nods but still feels a fleeting sting of discomfort in her stomach at that thought. Because staying at home wouldn't necessarily have helped, as she had the exact same feeling in her body when she sat at her robot mom's breakfast table. The feeling that something wasn't right.

Stop being such a drama queen, she orders herself, and for a while, it actually works. For a while, she manages to shake off the sensation.

Then they step in through the doorway to the classroom.

Normally the math class is a rather lively crowd (Miss Miller would probably choose a word like *frantic*), but right now, all the students are sitting on their chairs, their backs straight and their eyes fixed rigidly on the board. None of them saying a single word.

Background figures in a theater setting. That's the image that pops into Rose's head. Figures cut out of cardboard, like the ones they made for the nativity play when they were small.

For the fourth or fifth time this morning, her gaze instinctively finds Kitty, but this time it doesn't trigger smiles, eye rolls, or spontaneous laughter as they make eye contact. Instead, Rose gets her own uneasiness and confusion mirrored more clearly than she likes.

"You just made it, girls. Hurry up and take your seats."

The words come from Miss Miller. She is standing over by the window, slightly hunched with her lower back leaning against the sill and both hands resting on her thighs. Usually, that's how she stands at her table, but today she has handed over that spot to their invited guests, Sheriff Hodge and his young assistant.

Hodge has looked old for as long as Rose has known him, but somehow, he looks even older today. It's as if the wrinkled face beneath his sparse, light gray hair sags more than usual. It almost looks like a mask that sits a little too loosely on his face. The only thing that doesn't look old and worn out about him is the uniform. It is, as always, freshly ironed and spotless.

No, that's not true. The uniform isn't the only thing. His eyes don't look old either. In fact, they look eerily awake and vigilant. As if he expects all hell to break loose in the classroom at any moment and is ready to act at a split second's notice.

In the wake of that thought comes a realization that makes Rose feel very small and makes her cheeks flare up with a pink hue.

It's her and Kitty that those ice blue eyes are staring at. It's them he is waiting for.

Embarrassed, they take their bags off their backs and clutch them against their bellies as they sneak in among their schoolmates and find their seats in the middle of the room.

Mates might be a strong word right now. Because although most of them meet her gaze and return her awkward smile when she passes them, their smiles don't seem genuine. They seem put-on, like her mom's smile this morning.

Once Rose and Kitty have taken their seats, Miss Miller tiptoes over to their desks and holds out a small basket. In it lies a pile of phones.

"You know the rule when there is a guest lecture," she whispers.

Rose nods and Kitty sighs, after which they both pull out their phones and put them in the basket.

While Miss Miller walks back to her spot by the

window, Sheriff Hodge steps forward, clears his throat, and says:

"As I was about to say before I was interrupted, my name is Ben Hodge, and this is my assistant, Officer Emmanuel Mendez."

He gestures at Mendez, who sports a chalk-white Colgate smile and makes one of those little nods that really aren't more than a wink.

And despite her discomfort, it doesn't escape Rose's attention that Kitty was right. He is a good-looking man. Especially those eyes. Dark chocolate floating in caramel. That's the description that pops into her head.

Good-looking, yeah ... but also twice your age.

"We're here as part of a collaboration between the school and police districts," Hodge continues, "and we'd like to talk to you about some important issues."

He nods toward his assistant, who immediately raises his hand and points a small, white remote control at the ceiling. A second later, a faint beep sounds, followed by the lazy buzzing of the projector, and then the theme of the lecture appears on the whiteboard in large, curved WordArt letters.

PERSONAL SAFETY AND CRIME PREVENTION— AN INITIATIVE TO STRENGTHEN COMMUNITY AND HEALTHY VALUES AMONG YOUNG PEOPLE IN THE OAKWOOD SCHOOL DISTRICT.

"Obviously, personal safety is always important," Hodge says. "But especially at your age, you need be careful. And what do I mean by that?"

It's a rhetorical question, and he doesn't give them a chance to answer before he raises his voice and catches the ball himself.

"I'm referring, of course, to the fact that you've started going to parties and stay out later in the evening. In some cases, alcohol is also part of the equation. Therefore, it's important that you keep an eye on each other when out in the nightlife. Whenever possible, stick together in groups, stay away from dubious places, always be aware of your surroundings, and have a plan in case of emergencies."

On the board behind Hodge, the title text is replaced by a bulleted list containing his talking points ... but below the list is an image that doesn't fit the context at all—and that sends a chill down Rose's spine.

She looks over at Kitty, who shapes her lips into a silent but clear message:

What the hell is that?

The image shows an animal lying on a paved road. It looks like a cat, but it could also be a small dog. It's difficult to determine with absolute certainty, as the fur is disheveled and filled with clumps of coagulated blood, the animal's hind body is twisted

around itself, and its head is crushed beyond re-
cognition.

Rose opens her mouth to say something. Exactly
what, she doesn't know … but it doesn't matter
anyway, because nothing comes out. Her throat is
closed.

"However, looking out for one another isn't just
about taking care of your friends," Hodge continues in
a voice that sounds distant and muffled to Rose. As if
he is no longer standing inside the classroom but has
moved out on the other side of the window and is
talking to them from there. "It's also about making
sure that no one breaks the rules. So, if you see anything suspicious or spot a deviant, don't hesitate to
contact the police."

Spot a deviant? For some reason, this strange word-
ing sends another shiver down Rose's back. Especially
since she feels pretty sure Hodge's gaze flipped straight
to her and Kitty as he said it.

Her imagination? Could be. But that does not
change the fact that she feels more and more … what?
Cornered?

Up at the whiteboard, Hodge places his old, bony
hands on his hips like a man who has just completed a
construction project and is admiring the result. He also
smiles, as if he's proud.

Or as if he knows something they don't.

"Now some of you may be wondering how one recognizes a deviant," he says. "Luckily, it's easy. You see, deviants are hysterical. They love to create a panic, and they overreact when faced with things they don't understand."

He looks over at Officer Mendez, who nods and presses the remote once more.

Up on the board, the dead animal slips aside with a comical scroll animation that seems so inappropriate to Rose that she grimaces. She does the same when the next slide appears. Grimaces ... and brings her hands up in front of her mouth.

"What the hell is this?" she hears Kitty exclaim beside her, and instinctively she knows that it was a mistake. That her friend should have swallowed her indignation and kept it to herself. Not that her reaction is unreasonable, since the new image is even more gruesome than the previous one.

"A classic overreaction," Hodge says, nodding in Kitty's direction with an eerily condescending smile on his lips. "Sometimes an example is just the best explanation."

He glances at his colleague, and Mendez leaves his place at the whiteboard to march toward Kitty, who pushes her chair backward in fear.

"Hold on a sec," Rose starts, but she never gets any further in the sentence. This has two reasons;

Partly, she realizes that none of the other students seem to care in the slightest about either the bizarre presentation or Mendez' sudden, threatening behavior, and partly, she is interrupted by Hodge, who says:

"Well, I'll be darned. Two with one stone."

Now Officer Mendez stops in front of Kitty's table, fixing his gaze on her, then on Rose. His brown eyes no longer look alluring. They look like small, black marbles. The eyes of a bird of prey.

"I'm going to need you to come with me."

"Where, um ... where are we going?" Rose asks.

"Don't worry, you'll come back to the classroom later."

"That's not an answer," Kitty exclaims. "What if we prefer to stay here?"

The words express determination, but Kitty's voice quivers like a blade of grass in windy weather, and that drains all their power.

"Let's not make this more difficult than it needs to be," Mendez says, exposing his row of chalk-white teeth again. His smile, like his eyes, has lost all its charm.

"Is it just us?" Rose manages to stutter, after which she looks around at the other students in the class, hoping to find support.

There isn't much to come by. They observe her, yes,

but it's with eyes that express only mild interest and not a trace of compassion.

Slowly—and with a facial expression that doesn't hide his growing impatience—Officer Mendez leans forward and places a hand on the desk in front of Rose.

"For now, it's just the two of you," he hisses. "But my guess is you'll be joined by a couple more later. Does that answer your question, Miss ...?"

He makes a circular motion with his hand, urging her to complete the sentence, but Rose doesn't want to give him her name. In fact, it's the last thing in the world she feels like doing right now. Therefore, she drags out the moment and tries to avoid his drilling gaze.

"Lavine," a voice says over by the window. "Her name is Rose Lavine."

"Rose Lavine," Mendez repeats, slowly nodding his head up and down. "Thank you, Miss Miller."

Rose stares at her teacher in disbelief, and for reasons she doesn't fully understand, she feels deeply hurt and betrayed.

If Miss Miller registers her indignation, however, she doesn't let it show. She just continues shamelessly on to the next betrayal.

"And the girl next to her is Katherine Burns. She goes by Kitty."

Mendez nods and leans even further in over Rose's

desk. So far in that she can smell the eggs and bacon he got for breakfast as he sighs deeply, like he wants to emphasize how exhausting all of this is.

"You can leave your bags in here," he says. "You won't need them."

Rose wants to protest and tell him that they haven't even agreed to go with him. That she finds his behavior unprofessional and, frankly, quite menacing. The problem is that her throat is so constricted that she can't get a single word out.

But that's not even the worst part. The worst part is that the same seems to apply to her friend. Big-mouthed Kitty, who usually has a comeback for everything, is paralyzed and silent as the grave.

"We don't have all day, girls."

Although he speaks more calmly than his younger colleague, there's something in old Sheriff Hodge's voice that makes them both jerk uneasily in their chairs before they get up and reluctantly follow Officer Mendez out of the classroom.

On the way to the door, both Rose and Kitty have their eyes fixed on their feet, but before they walk out into the hallway, Rose lifts her head and takes one last look around. First at the students, who have now lost interest in the interruption and turned their gaze back to the guest lecturer, then at the whiteboard, where the image that, according to Hodges, caused them to overreact still resides.

The picture is of a young woman who—just like the dead animal on the previous slide—lies lifeless on a paved road and has had her head reduced to a lumpy mass of hair, skin, and dried-out blood.

Chapter Four

Halloween is a big deal at Oakwood High. Everyone loves the annual celebration of the holiday, and usually, preparations for it already start during the first week of October.

This year is no exception. The music class has been rehearsing a new version of Michael Jackson's *Thriller* every day for the last two weeks, and the drama crew has begun decorating for the party. Therefore, the exercise bars mounted on the walls of the gym are adorned with artificial cobwebs, and on a table in the center of the hall stands a giant spider, made with black-painted papier-mâché, twine, and steel wire.

At this moment, Rose is staring at that very same spider. Because it's the gym they've been ushered into —and it's here, inside the penalty field of the basketball court on the worn, reddish-brown floor planks, that Officer Mendez has told them to sit down.

Rose doesn't want to sit on the floor, but she also doesn't feel like testing what would happen if she refused. Because she no longer doubts that the officer's intentions aren't good, and her confusion has gradually turned into fear.

"What are we supposed to do here?" Kitty asks as they sit down on the hard floor. "There's nobody in here."

"Wait," Mendez replies coldly.

"For what?"

"For me to come back," Mendez says even colder, after which he starts to turn away. Halfway into the movement, however, he hesitates and looks at them once more. "And you stay put. Is that clear?"

Kitty opens her mouth to protest, but Rose stops her by placing a hand on her forearm.

"Is that clear?" Mendez repeats.

"Of course," Rose says. She tries to conceal her anxiety and sound natural, but she isn't sure whether or not she succeeds.

For how long Officer Mendez stays there, towering over them with his arms crossed and the analyzing gaze of his black birds-of-prey-eyes locked on her, Rose doesn't know, but it feels like an eternity. So, it's a great relief when he finally nods and starts walking back in the direction of the double door where they entered.

The relief is short-lived, though, because just before he grabs the handle, he stops as if remembering something.

For a moment, Rose fears that he has changed his mind and has decided to stay in here with them, but when the sound of his steps on the creaking planks once again fills the empty hall, it's not them he is moving toward. It's the stage down at the end—or rather; the area behind the stage.

"This is so fucked up," Kitty whispers as he disappears out of sight. "As soon as we're sure he's gone, we're getting the hell out of here. You with me, Red?"

Rose nods, but mostly as a reflex response ... because something has set off another alarm in the back of her mind, and that's what has her attention right now. It's the feeling that she has seen something important. She just can't quite figure out what it is.

Suddenly, it becomes crystal clear, and she feels her stomach tighten.

The area behind the stage ... where the only other exit from the gym is located.

"He's going to lock us up," she whispers, half to Kitty, half to herself.

"What's that?"

"He wants to lock us up," Rose repeats.

Kitty stares at her as the comprehension slowly dawns in her eyes.

"But he, um ... he doesn't have keys to the gym, does he?"

That is a fair point. Nevertheless, Rose feels pretty confident that she's right. And when, a second later, she hears two loud clicks and then a heavy, metallic rattle from behind the stage—like when someone pulls the chain to check if the bike is properly secured to the rack—the last shred of doubt disappears from her mind. She also has a pretty good idea as to what might have made that sound.

Now, Officer Mendez reappears on the right side of the stage, and as she had predicted, his handcuffs are no longer hanging from his belt.

"He can't just do this," Kitty says. She starts in a whisper, but gradually, both the level of anger and volume in her voice increase.

"Kitty, don't," Rose tries, but it's too late. Her friend is well known for her temper and her sharp tongue, and both have been suppressed for too long now.

"HEY! I'M TALKING TO YOU!" she shouts, after which she, lacking a better object, pulls her pearl bracelet off her wrist and hurls it at the officer. It misses the target, by far, and ends up under one of the wall bars on the right side after a long slide across the floor. "YOU CAN'T JUST LEAVE US IN HERE!"

Officer Mendez hesitates for a moment, his gaze sliding back and forth between the bracelet and its sender. Then he shakes his head and continues toward the door.

Knowing what effect that response will have on her friend, Rose reaches for Kitty's arm, but once more she is too slow. Kitty, already halfway up, jumps the rest of the way, then marches over to the officer.

"YOU MAY BE A COP, BUT I DON'T CARE. YOU CAN'T TREAT PEOPLE LIKE THAT. IT'S TOTALLY—"

The smack is deafening in the big, empty gym hall. It reverberates through the room, tearing the air apart and resounding in every corner.

Rose can almost feel the slap on her own cheek, as if it were her face that had been hit. Not just the burning, physical pain but also the emotional one. The humiliation. The shock.

Dumbstruck, she stares at her friend, who is now staggering backward away from the officer while clutching her face.

"You ... hit me?" she murmurs, then turning to Rose. "He hit me."

"I told you to stay put," the officer snarls. "You call that staying put? Marching over here like that, yelling at me?"

He lifts his index finger and takes a breath, as if

about to say something more, but then lowers it and shakes his head instead.

"It's not even worth it. It's like talking to a door. Fucking deviants. Can't even follow basic instructions."

With this low-key expression of his annoyance, Officer Mendez turns his back on them and strides out of the hall at a rapid pace. Almost as if he wants to accentuate how offended he feels.

"He's insane," Kitty sobs as the doors slam shut behind him. "Oh God, Red. He's totally insane."

As a fateful underlining of those words, a series of creaking and rattling noises arise from the other side of the double door. Noises that trigger panic in Rose because they can only mean one thing:

All exits from Oakwood High's gym hall have now been closed off.

Chapter Five

If it goes wrong, chances are that it will go *very* wrong. Both Rose and Kitty know this. But they have to do something, and since the windows in the locker room are blocked off with cast-iron bars that won't budge an inch, they'll have to try the windows inside the gym.

The problem is that said windows are placed about five feet above the exercise bars on the walls, which means that Rose will have to stand on the top bar to pry open a window. And even if that part of the project were to succeed, she would still have to jump down on the other side. How far is that? Twelve feet? And it's not soft grass on the ground out there. It's asphalt.

Now you just take one step at a time, she tells herself as she grabs two of the middle bars and starts climbing up. *First you need to get up to the window.*

"Be careful, Red," she hears Kitty whisper behind her.

She sounds hoarse. That's no wonder, though, considering that their first attempt at getting out of the gym consisted of screaming—very loudly, very persistently, and very much in vain—for help.

"I'll be careful," Rose replies. "I just wish they weren't so slippery."

What she really means is that she wishes her hands weren't so clammy. But it's a condition she can't do anything about. Because she's deeply frightened—and with that inevitably comes a pair of sweaty palms.

The wood creaks disturbingly as she closes her fingers around the top bar of the exercise ladder and hesitantly initiates the final part of this nerve-wracking balance exercise. She starts by moving her upper body up over the top bar so she can rest her elbow on it and press one shoulder against the wall for support. Then she slowly leans to the side until she is able to lift her foot up high enough to step on the top bar. Once her left foot is securely positioned, she shifts her weight to the opposite side and pulls her right foot up to join it.

One ... two ... three deep breaths through a mouth that feels completely dried out before she finds the courage to move her hands onto the wall—where there's nothing to grab ahold of—and push off with her feet.

Fear forces her eyes shut, and for a moment the scraping sound of her sweater rubbing against the wall is the only confirmation that she hasn't fallen backward. For even though she knows she's pressing everything she can against the wall—knees, hands, elbows, shoulders, and cheek—her body is numb. It's as if every neural route has been scorched. Charred by terror.

However, once she opens her eyes, all the threads join again. She feels her body quivering, and it also seems like the bar beneath her feet is following suit. It certainly creaks alarmingly.

"Breathe slowly," Kitty suggests from the floor. It's a well-meant—and in fact quite sensible—piece of advice, but Rose has to bite her lip to keep from barking at her. To resist the urge to ask Kitty if she would like to swap places since she's so full of great ideas.

She turns her gaze upward. Her eyeball measure says she should be able to reach the handle of the window ... but it also says she will have to stretch her arm all the way up over her head to do it. She might even need to stand on her toes.

"Just get on with it," she whispers to herself, yet

she just stands there, pressed against the wall as if she were nailed to it. A ridiculous teenage girl version of the Savior on the cross. She just won't save anyone as long as she—

An unexpected tremble goes through the bars beneath her feet, and she frantically moves her arms up and down in semicircles on the wall to maintain her balance.

"Oh shit, sorry," says Kitty, who is climbing up the bars to keep her company. "I didn't mean to scare you. I just had an idea."

"It had better be good," Rose mumbles.

The answer comes, not in the form of words, but through a physical gesture as Kitty places a hand on Rose's lower leg. And while this extra support probably wouldn't make a real difference if she actually lost her balance, it's reassuring to feel her friend's presence physically.

Inch by inch, Rose's right hand begins to work its way up the wall toward the window, while the left moves downward as a counterweight on the opposite side.

Suddenly, she feels it against her fingertips; the cold metal of the handle. She tries to push it upward but quickly realizes that her suspicion, unfortunately, was correct. She will have to get on her toes if she wants it opened.

"You've got me?"

"I've got you, Rose."

As she says this, Kitty puts a little extra pressure on Rose's leg. Undoubtedly, this is to accentuate that she means what she says, and it *is* a reassuring gesture. Still, it's her choice of words that reassures Rose the most. Because this is the first time in years that Kitty has used her first name instead of calling her *Red*, and somehow that stresses the gravity.

Aware that she needs to act while she still has the courage, Rose moves her feet backward, making her toes rest on the middle of the bar, and pushes off.

"It's working," she exclaims as she feels the cold metal slide into the palm of her hand. And it is true. This time, the handle swings all the way up when she pushes it.

A squeak sounds as the rubber strip lets go of the frame and the window swings outward. Simultaneously, an icy breeze draws in. It crawls down Rose's neck, behind the collar of her shirt, and down her back. Her body's instinctive response is to curl into a fetal position, but she resists the urge. She's come this far, and she's not planning on giving up now.

She moves her hand to the left and grabs the bottom edge of the window frame. Next, she moves her other hand up and does the same with it.

"I might need a push," she says as she places one foot on the wall and prepares to pull herself up.

Below her, Kitty slides one arm in under the top bar, locking herself at the elbow. Then she nods at Rose.

"You can step on my shoulder ... and, Red?"

"Yeah?"

"You've got this."

I sure hope you're right, Kitty, Rose thinks, but she doesn't say anything, because now her focus is on the task. On getting up to that stupid window.

She tightens her grip on the frame, engages all the muscles that her brain allows her to control ... and then she pulls herself upward.

It stings in her arms, her sneakers slip perilously on the wall twice, and there isn't a trace of grace in her ascent ... but she makes it. She pulls herself far enough up to edge her upper arms over the frame—and after a short rest, she continues fighting her way up until she is perched in the window opening, her legs straddling the frame on each side.

It's a long way down. Long enough to evoke a sense of vertigo.

The harsh October wind doesn't exactly help either. It swirls around her in an unpredictable rhythm, pushing and pulling without warning.

"Do you see anyone?" Kitty asks.

Although she has already done so several times with the same result, Rose lets her gaze drift across the parking lot outside the window before responding with a resigned shake of the head.

Rain-soaked asphalt and empty cars. That's all. No people. No help. The only sounds are distant traffic from the main road, the wind, and the icy raindrops constantly tapping on the window.

"God damnit!" Kitty exclaims. A statement with which Rose can only agree: "What the hell do we do then? How far down is it?"

"Too far to jump, but maybe I can lower myself down the wall first so the distance will be shorter. It's just ... it's pretty wet."

She leans down and touches a part of the wall that is outside the window's protection. Just as she suspected, it's quite slippery.

"If it's too risky, don't do it."

That's great, Kitty, but we can't exactly sit around and wait for Officer Friendly to come back either, can we? Rose thinks, but she doesn't say that out loud either. Instead, she grabs the window frame with both hands and tugs on it a few times as if to check whether it's strong enough to support her weight. Then she pulls her right leg up and moves it out over the frame, thus placing both legs on the outside of the wall.

Her sneakers have rubber soles. If she's lucky, they

might provide enough traction to counteract the slippery surface of the wet bricks. This is what she hopes as she turns around on her stomach, places her feet on the wall, and starts lowering herself downward.

She's *not* lucky. Hardly has she pushed herself over the edge of the frame before the tips of her shoes slide down the wall with a shrill screech, and her chest slams against the bricks—so hard that she can barely maintain her grip on the frame.

"What's happening?" sounds on the other side. "Red? Are you okay?"

"Y-yeah, I'm okay," Rose stammers. "My feet slipped. I ... I don't know if I can climb down it, Kitty."

A pause. Then Kitty's voice returns:

"It's okay. We'll figure something out. Can you climb back up?"

Rose looks up at the window frame, then down at her shoes, and finally at the wall. She doesn't need to get that far up, and there's a strip to her left where the bricks are dry. If she's able to push off with her feet there, it might actually work.

Following this plan, she puts her foot on the wall and tightens her grip on the frame. Then she pulls, kicks, and moans in turn until she is high enough up to climb in over the window frame.

Hanging there on her stomach, her vision starts to

blur and wobble. As if she is on the verge of losing consciousness.

That might very well have happened. She could easily have gone out like a light, lying exhausted and flaccid across the lower edge of the window frame.

She could ... if it hadn't been for the sound of the car turning into the parking lot.

Chapter Six

The car is a silver Kia Sorento. It belongs to Kristal Shanahan, who is one of the teachers at Oakwood High —and who now gets out of the vehicle and unfolds a peach-colored umbrella with black polka dots.

Other than her name, Rose doesn't know much about Mrs. Shanahan. Partly because she has only had two classes with her as a substitute when her usual literature teacher was sick, and partly because Mrs. Shanahan is a fairly new addition to the teaching staff at Oakwood. She transferred from Kansas and only joined the school last year.

But despite the limited acquaintance, Rose at this moment feels like she is spotting an old friend.

Judging by the expression on Mrs. Shanahan's face, the feeling isn't exactly mutual. It's not the joy of reunion that she radiates as she spots the teenager up in the window. It is shock and indignation.

"What on earth do you think you're doing? Get down from there!"

For a moment, Rose is unable to answer at all. She just stares at the teacher as she comes closer and stops seven or eight feet away from the wall, shaking her head.

"It's not our fault," Rose exclaims, but hearing how dumb that explanation sounds, she corrects it to: "It was the cop. He locked us in the gym, and we can't get out."

"The cop?" the teacher says, squinting her eyes and looking around as if trying to determine whether she has been the target of a prank. "What is this? Where is your teacher?"

"I'm not lying," Rose says, struggling to hold back the tears. "We've been locked in the gym by a police officer. He's crazy and he ... he hit Kitty! Could you please get us out before he comes back?"

Maybe it's the distress in Rose's voice, maybe it's the information that Kitty has been hurt. Whatever it is, it triggers a change in the teacher's eyes. She is still skeptical, that's obvious, but it is no longer pure distrust toward them.

"I'll come in there," she says after considering it for a moment. "But I swear, if this turns out to be a joke ..."

"It's not," Rose replies promptly. "I promise, Mrs. Shanahan."

"Yeah, we'll see," the teacher says, after which she tilts the umbrella up from her shoulder so Rose can no longer see her face. Then she runs across the parking lot in the direction of one of the school's back entrances.

"Is she coming?"

Rose nods, and Kitty lets out a sigh of relief, then buries her face in her hands.

Rose does the same; presses her face into her palms, sobbing and chuckling at the same time. It's as if a floodgate has been opened now that she knows help is on the way. As if the accumulated emotions can finally be allowed to—

A movement out in the parking lot—something she catches peripherally between her fingers—makes her stiffen. She lowers her hands and feels her heart sink with them.

It's him. Officer Mendez. He has just stepped out of a door at the opposite end and is now sprinting across the empty parking lot.

And he is heading toward the door that their rescuer has just entered.

"We need to warn her," Rose cries, looking down at Kitty. "She's on her way in here, and he's following her."

"Mendez?" Kitty asks, and when Rose replies with a nod, she turns pale. "Shit, shit, shit! What do we do?"

The high-pitched tone of Kitty's voice reveals that she's on the verge of a breakdown, and Rose realizes it's her turn to keep a cool head.

"You run to the door, and as soon as you hear her outside, you tell her to hide until he's gone. Got it?"

"But then what about you? If he comes in here and you're still up there—"

"Never mind that. I'm coming down now. Besides, I think he already saw me."

"But—"

"NOW, KITTY!"

Rose's outburst makes Kitty jolt. But it works; she turns around and runs in the direction of the entrance to the gym.

In the meantime, Rose starts to crawl down from the window. She does it quickly but cautiously, and luckily, getting down is easier than getting up. The only thing that really causes her problems is the moment when she has to let go of the frame and find her balance on the top bar of the exercise ladder. She handles the rest without much trouble.

The very second that Rose sets foot on the gym's floor planks again, the teacher arrives at the gym's entrance. At least judging from the rattle coming from over there, as if someone is tugging at the double door

... or maybe trying to remove the things used to lock it. Right after follows the sound of Kitty's voice:

"Mrs. Shanahan? Can you hear me?"

"I hear you, yes. I'll get you out. I just need to remove this."

"No, you have to get away from the door!" Kitty and Rose shout in chorus. "You need to hide!"

For a moment, it's completely quiet outside the door. Then the teacher's voice returns.

"Listen, what is this, girls? Can you make up your minds? First you want me to let you out, and now you want me gone?"

"He's coming," Rose tries. "The officer. He followed you over here."

"Look, I'm coming in there, and then you're going to tell me—"

She doesn't get any further before two sounds interrupt her. Two sounds that paint an all too clear picture of what has occurred on the other side of the door.

The first sound is a thud. Like when you slap a hand against your thigh—or like when you smack a blunt object into the back of another person's head.

The second sound is much louder. It's the sound of something big, like a person, tilting over and crashing into a door or a wall.

"Mrs. Shanahan?" Rose asks, but her voice is so

muffled and weak that she's probably the only one able to hear it. "Mrs. Shanahan?"

No answer. Only a soft dragging sound followed by a faint rustle as someone starts to remove things on the other side again.

Rose and Kitty look at each other nervously, then back away from the door.

Slowly, it opens, and the first thing to meet them is the sight of Mrs. Shanahan's hand. It falls in through the crack and lands limply to the floor. Next follows her head, covered by disheveled hair, because she hangs in the air eight inches above the ground.

She is *dragged* in by the policeman. He is grabbing the side of her winter coat and lugging her across the floor. As if she were a sack of garbage.

As the officer lets go and drops the unconscious teacher on the floor, Rose notices a glossy, dark red spot in the back of her head—and for a moment this threatens to trigger another panic attack in her.

Because in a fleeting moment, she doesn't just see Mrs. Shanahan. She also sees the woman who was in the image on the whiteboard. The lifeless woman whose face had been trampled, reduced to a lumpy mass of hair, skin, and clotted blood.

Is that the fate that awaits them?

"Why are you doing this to us?" she hears Kitty ask

in a voice that is hollow and shaky. "What is it you want?"

Mendez stares at her, slightly raised eyebrows, the hint of a smile.

"Don't worry, you'll get out of here," he says. "We just need to make sure we get all of them."

Although she doesn't know why, those words make the hairs on Rose's neck stand up. Perhaps it's because the timbre of his voice makes it sound like a threat. A *serious* threat.

"All of who?"

Part of her already knows the answer, but Rose needs to ask. Needs to hear him say it out loud. Get him to confirm her suspicions.

And when he does, she feels hope draining away from her heart as if it were water spiraling down a sink.

"All the deviants, of course," is the answer the officer gives.

Chapter Seven

When Mrs. Shanahan finally regains consciousness, the officer has long since left the gym—and locked the doors behind him, of course. However, out of sight certainly doesn't mean out of mind in this case, and Rose is fully aware that it's only a matter of time before he'll be back.

"What ... happened?" the teacher asks, moving her hand to the back of her head. When it reappears, two of the fingers are red.

"He knocked you out," says Kitty, who is also kneeling on the floor next to Mrs. Shanahan just on the other side. "We think he snuck up on you while you were trying to get the doors open."

For a moment, there is nothing but blank confusion in the teacher's hazel eyes. Then the comprehension hits her, and she sits up with a jerk.

"Locked," Rose says, seeing Mrs. Shanahan's gaze move toward the entrance doors. "That one and the door behind the stage too."

"You said it was a police officer who did this?"

"A psycho officer," Kitty confirms. "There is something seriously wrong with him. He—"

"Not just him," Rose interrupts. "He did this, sure. But there is also something wrong with everyone else. They just don't ... care."

"What do you mean?"

"The officers, Sheriff Hodge and his assistant, put a PowerPoint up on the whiteboard in our class with a picture of a dead woman. A really disgusting picture— and the only ones who reacted to it were Kitty and me. The rest were completely indifferent."

Like your mom this morning, a mocking voice whispers in Rose's head, and she has to concentrate to push it into the background.

For a long time, the teacher says nothing. She just sits completely still on the floor, her drowsy eyes flitting back and forth between Rose and Kitty.

"I ... believe you," she says at last, although Rose has the feeling that those words are mostly Mrs. Shanahan talking to herself. "Actually, I experienced something like that when I was on my way in here. I passed George, the janitor, out in the hallway. He asked why I was in such a hurry, and I told him about you—that you were locked in the gym—and he was completely unaffected by it."

She hesitates a little, then lets out a sound that is somewhere between a snort and a chuckle.

"I actually think he wished me a good day. That's just … nuts."

Rose opens her mouth to agree, but before she can say anything, she is interrupted as the teacher frantically starts to look around, on her hips, her shoulders, and on the floor.

"What's the matter?"

"My bag. I had a bag. My cell phone was in it."

"I think he took it," Rose says. "You didn't have a bag when he … carried you in here."

The teacher clenches her hands, bends her head forward, and closes her eyes.

"Excuse me, girls," she then says, "but *fuck* and *shit*!"

"It's okay, Mrs. Shanahan," Rose says, giving her a frozen smile. "Besides, you're totally right. This *is* a shitty situation."

For a while, those words are left hanging in the air in the large, empty gym hall, as if they were the closing sentence of a play. Then Rose puts her hands on the floor and pushes herself up.

"We can't get the doors open, calling for help doesn't work, and the window thing wasn't a success either." Kitty sighs. "So, what do we do now?"

"We'll figure something out, girls," Mrs. Shanahan says. She sounds more composed now. Maybe it's just a role she's stepping into, but it doesn't matter. Rose is just grateful to have an adult to lean on—even if it probably doesn't make any real difference to their situation.

But then again, the newcomer is able give them some information that they didn't have before.

"How were the doors locked out there?" she asks. "He wedged something in behind the handles, right?"

Mrs. Shanahan nods.

"Gardening tools. I'm guessing he just took a random pile from the janitor's storage room. It's right down the stairs out there."

"Wood or metal?"

The teacher looks at her with a thoughtful expression in her eyes. Then she nods.

"It's going to take a lot of force."

"There are three of us," Rose replies, after which she points to the Halloween decoration with the big spider in the center of the hall. "And we can use the table as a battering ram."

Mrs. Shanahan lets her gaze wander over to the table and from there back to the double doors. So does Kitty. Then they both nod.

Chapter Eight

Every impact reverberates. Not only in the gym hall but also in Rose's body. It sounds like thunder and feels like an earthquake, the tremors of which can be felt in her bones every time their improvised battering ram crashes into the double door. And it also causes a wave of dread in her every single time. Dread that the noise will reveal them.

But she'll simply have to swallow her fear. Because it works. What started as a gap of less than an inch has now turned into an opening of almost four. And two of the gardening tools that are fastened behind the handle of the doors have already broken in half.

"Again!" she hears behind her. "We're almost there!"

It's Mrs. Shanahan. She is holding the back two

legs of the table, while Rose has the front two. They're doing the heavy lifting while Kitty's primary task is to keep the tabletop balanced. They chose to distribute the tasks that way as they quickly realized that the battering ram was more effective if the table was vertical. Moreover, it made sense, since Rose has always been a lot stronger than Kitty—and Mrs. Shanahan is also in surprisingly good shape, even though Rose guesses that she's in her forties.

"Now, one more time with full force!"

Rose nods, tightens her grip, and swings the table as hard as she can.

Two sharp cracks emerge from the crevice as the wooden handles of the two remaining tools—a rake and an old axe—break, and the doors swing outward at such speed that Rose and the teacher are on the verge of tumbling forward. It could easily have resulted in a bone fracture, because there are only about six feet between the door and the staircase that leads down to the janitor's tool room in the basement.

"You did it!" Kitty exclaims as the other two put the table down on the floor. "You actually freaking did it! We got out!"

Rose wipes sweat off her forehead and nods but says nothing. She needs a moment to catch her breath … and to prepare for the next part.

Apparently, the teacher has no such need. She has

already moved on and has picked up one half of the broken rake. The half that still has the head attached, mind you.

The good Mrs. Shanahan is tougher than her appearance gives her credit for, Rose concludes, when she sees the teacher doing a test swing in the air with her improvised weapon.

"Hey, Mrs. Shan," Kitty says. "Does your bag have Halloween pictures on it?"

"Yeah, did you find it?"

Kitty responds by raising her hand and pointing toward the corner behind the open door. There lies a bag matching the description. It's upside down and it's almost folded into the corner as if it has been hurled there with great force.

The teacher bends down, picks it up, and rifles through it for a moment, then shakes her head.

"No cell phone?" Rose asks.

"No cell phone," Mrs. Shanahan replies. "But at least he didn't take my car keys."

She pauses to think, then points to the section of the stairs that leads up to the school's central corridor and says:

"When we get up there, I'll take the lead. And you let me do the talking if necessary, okay?"

"No argument here," Kitty says.

"Fine with me," Rose adds.

"Good, then let's do it."

The hallway is completely empty. Actually, it's not that strange, since everyone has classes at this time of day. Still, Rose gradually becomes more and more anxious as the hallway's lockers, posters, and closed doors glide by at the edge of her field of vision.

It's the silence. It has to be. It's so quiet in here that the sound of their own steps is all they can hear.

With that realization comes another: This hallway is never that quiet during school hours. *Never.* At a minimum, you should be able to hear a faint buzzing from inside the classrooms.

She turns around to pass this observation on to Kitty but doesn't have time to say anything before the silence is broken by a loud and shrill ringing.

The school bell. Any second now, the doors will be pulled open, and all the students will come rushing out into the hallway.

She exchanges a glance with the two others, who both answer with the same wavering shrug. And they are right. They've got no exits at hand and no obvious place to hide, so maybe it's better to stay put and let themselves be swallowed by the crowd.

Now the doors start to open, but ... they're not pulled open? They're opened quietly—and what ensues isn't the usual stampede of teens falling over each other in their eagerness to get away. The students

PER JACOBSEN

are there, but they're walking calmly and quietly. No running, no pushing, and no shouting. They stroll in small, eerily synchronous groups, chatting with each other. Friendly and politely, like the two bullies and the nerd with the binder this morning.

Rose jolts as something touches her arm. She spins around and is greeted by Kitty's green eyes. They are as full of concern as she feels.

"Come on, Red," she says. "We'll walk with them, nice and easy, until we're at the exit."

Rose nods but still isn't able to move until Mrs. Shanahan places her hand on her back and gives her a gentle push.

Hesitantly, she starts walking. She tries to follow the underlying rhythm of the flock, which she can sense is there but can't quite catch.

These are her peers. Many of them are her friends. Yet right now, she doesn't feel like part of the group. Right now, she feels like a gazelle who has strayed into lions' territory by accident. And she knows it's irrational, that it's her imagination running wild, but she can't help but think that they might suddenly stop, point at the deviants, and yell for the officers to come.

That doesn't happen. The flock continues their calm march toward the school canteen. Even when Rose discreetly signals the other two and then starts to change direction, none of the students react.

76

"What are you doing?" Kitty whispers. "The exit is that way."

"I know, but the classrooms are empty now and our phones are still inside ours."

"But what if he's in there?"

"We'll check if the coast is clear first, of course."

Kitty's eyes narrow and tiny furrows appear on her forehead. Then she nods reluctantly. So does Mrs. Shanahan.

The door to their classroom is ajar, and once they've reached it, Rose glances through the opening.

No students, no teachers—and most importantly, no police officers. So far, so good.

She lets her gaze drift over to the window and, to her relief, finds that the little wicker basket is still on the sill where Miss Miller left it after collecting their cell phones.

"Can you keep watch out here?" she whispers.

"Okay," Kitty replies. "Take mine too, okay?"

"I will."

After those words, Rose gently pries open the door and steps inside. Once in, she edges her way past the tables and moves to the window.

Locating the cell phones she's looking for isn't difficult, as they were the last two to be collected, which means they're at the top of the pile.

She puts Kitty's phone in her pocket. She's about to

do the same with her own, but she hesitates when she spots the little blue light flashing next to the camera lens. The notification light.

It's probably nothing. The phone company sending her some stupid offer or something like that. Definitely nothing.

But.

She brings the phone to life with a press of the *Home* button, then swipes the lock screen away.

11 MISSED CALLS: SEBASTIAN

For a while, Rose's brain is unable to decode the words and extract a meaningful context. Her hands, however, seem to get it almost instantly. They start shaking uncontrollably, so she has to press the phone against her stomach to keep from dropping it.

What could be so important that her little brother —for the first time ever—chooses to call her during school hours? And so important that he didn't stop after the first or second attempt but chose to call *eleven* times?

It's connected. Somehow, all of it is connected. The madness at her school today and Sebastian's calls are connected to each other.

It's not just a gut feeling. She knows, beyond a shadow of a doubt, that something is very, very wrong with a lot of people today—and the missed calls tell her that something is also going on at her little brother's school.

With a finger she can barely control, she opens her phone's contact list, scrolls down to Sebastian's name, and taps *Call*.

One ... two ... three ... four ... five ... six ... seven long dial tones. Then a short click sounds, and a voice breaks through. But it's not the voice of her little brother. It's a woman's voice.

"You're trying to reach the phone number ... 555-323-4867. The recipient is currently unavailable. Please try again later or press *one* to leave a message."

Over by the door to the classroom, three small knocks sound. Rose looks over there and sees Kitty making a circular *get a move on* motion with her hand.

Rose replies with a nod and a raised thumb, then turns her attention back to the screen, where she presses one.

"Sebastian?" she whispers. "When you get this, please call me back right away. I didn't have my phone before, but I do now. And, um, Sebastian, if any ... weird stuff is going on at your school, you just get out of there, okay? Just go home or something. I'll take the blame if Mom ..."

The answering machine's end tone hasn't sounded yet, so she could have finished the sentence. There would have been plenty of time for it on the recording.

But at that very moment, Rose spots the officers outside the window. And what she sees them doing causes her to end the message on her little brother's voicemail in a completely different way than she had planned.

"No, what are they doing?" are her final words in the message. "Oh God! What are they *doing* to him?"

Chapter Nine

In the center of the outdoor area in front of Oakwood High stands a sculpture. It's made of iron and depicts a large tree whose branches are covered with small graduation caps instead of leaves. The tree was a gift to the school from Elijah Kanvas, a former student who became successful as an artist and wanted to give something back to the place that helped him hone his talent.

As stated on the bronze plaque on the sculpture's platform, the tree is intended as a daily reminder to students that their dreams can come true if they accept the gift of learning.

However, as of this moment, there is one student whose dreams certainly won't come true. It's the boy that Rose noticed earlier in the day because he was the only one who, like her and Kitty, ran from the bus to the school entrance to get shelter from the rain. The boy with the *I PAUSED MY GAME TO BE HERE* hoodie.

And the reason why his dreams won't come true?

He is no longer alive. If he is, it would be nothing short of a miracle, given that his head has been twisted so far around his back that his flabby jaw rests on his left shoulder blade.

He is hanging up in the iron tree, his arms and one leg resting on different branches as if he were climbing and suddenly just died.

Except this wasn't sudden. Because he has been assaulted. Beaten to a pulp. His face is swollen, and the skin on his cheek is frayed and smeared with blood.

There is also a long red trail running across the wet tiles in front of the tree. All signs indicate that he has been hauled carelessly across the ground without anyone bothering to protect his head.

It's not just the tiles that have gotten a touch of red. So have the two artists, who decided to expand upon the original work by hanging up a lifeless teenager. Their hands are red, painted by the boy's blood. That doesn't seem to bother them in the slightest, though. They just stand there, side by side in the pouring rain, completely laidback, staring at the tree. Admiring their work as if they were two DIY enthusiasts who have just finished building a gazebo.

Old Sheriff Hodge and his assistant, Mendez.

Rose stares at them. She can't help it, even though she knows that the smart thing to do would be to back away from the window and run. To find Sebastian and run as far away as possible without looking back.

So do it already! Get a move on!

No. Her brain refuses to cooperate. It keeps her feet locked to the floor and her gaze locked on the two uniformed killers.

But it's not just them. There are others out there as well. A group of students from the school, standing under a canopy in the green area on the right side of the entrance. Three of them are leaning against a bike rack, chatting away, while the last one munches on a sandwich—without even blinking at the sight of his dead schoolmate in the iron tree.

Come on! Back away and leave!

Rose almost screams as a white hand shoots forth at the edge of her field of vision and grabs her arm.

"Hey," Kitty whispers. "We've been calling for you. We need to … oh, fuck."

For a moment, Kitty's voice dies out as if someone has pressed an *off* button inside her brain, but unlike Rose, she doesn't linger in the catatonic state. Instead, she starts pulling Rose's arm as she backs toward the door.

"We need to get out of here, Red. Now!"

"He's ... dead," Rose hears herself respond in a faint, trembling voice. "They killed him."

"I know—and that's exactly why we need to leave. Mrs. Shan's car is still in the parking lot behind the school, so we'll take the back exit."

"The cops killed that boy," Rose repeats, as if she thinks her friend either didn't understand the message or maybe didn't hear her the first time.

Kitty's answer is silent. She just pulls harder on Rose's arm. So hard that she almost stumbles—which actually turns out to be a good thing, as it shakes her out of her state of shock and enables her to move on her own.

Just over halfway through the classroom. That's as far as they get before old Hodge suddenly looks back over his shoulder.

His eyes are squinted, as if he senses something is going on but can't quite figure out what it is. He stays that way for a moment—and in that moment, Rose allows herself to hope that the sparse daylight out there reflects in the glass of the window, preventing him from looking into the classroom.

Then the moment ends, and Hodge grabs his assistant's elbow with one hand while lifting the other and pointing toward the window.

Toward them.

Chapter Ten

The rain has only gotten worse during the morning, so when they open the door and run out onto the stairs to the parking lot at the back of the school, both Rose and Kitty are on the verge of slipping on the wet steps.

Nevertheless, none of them slow down. Because whether it would be a sprained ankle or a broken arm that a fall would result in, one thing is certain: It would be preferable to getting caught by their pursuers.

"It's over there," Mrs. Shanahan groans, pointing. "It's the silver Kia. At the end."

Rose doesn't listen. Her body is on autopilot, following on the heels of the teacher across asphalt and through puddles, but her mind hasn't quite caught up yet. It's still stuck inside the classroom, struggling to comprehend the two findings that hit her like an earthquake.

The boy in the iron tree. The missed calls from her little brother. Her little brother, the one she has looked her mom in the eye every morning and promised that she will take care of. What if—

No! Don't you dare go down that road! Sebastian is fine!

She's pulled out of her stream of thought when Mrs. Shanahan takes out the car's remote control from her Halloween bag, presses it—and gets a response in the shape of a short beep followed by two flashes from the taillights.

"Get in," the teacher says, but before Rose does that, she hesitates for a moment, looking back over her shoulder.

Still no officers in sight. It feels wrong. It feels ... too easy?

"Rose! Come on!" Kitty roars. She's already sitting in the back seat, holding the door open for her. "We gotta go!"

"Yeah ... yeah, sorry. I'm coming."

As soon as Rose has taken a seat in the back, Mrs. Shanahan starts driving out of the parking lot—and as she does, Rose notices a detail she doesn't like.

The teacher's hands on the steering wheel. Mrs. Shanahan is the adult, and so far, she has lived up to that role by staying calm and taking the lead. But the hands expose her. They are shivering, and her knuckles have turned white because she clutches the steering wheel so hard.

She is struggling to hide it, yes, but Mrs. Shanahan is on the verge of collapse. And that's no wonder. Especially since Rose also notices another detail about those hands.

The ring. Mrs. Shanahan is married, probably also has children at home ... and just like Rose is worried about Sebastian, the teacher must be going out of her mind if that's the case.

"Where are we going?" Kitty asks.

"I need to get to Coulton," Rose says. "My little brother's school is there, and I ... um, I think he's in trouble too. He's tried to call me."

She is aware of how selfish it must seem, her attempting to put her own needs first like this, but she wouldn't be able to live with herself if she didn't try. Because she feels, deep in her heart, that it's true. That Sebastian needs her and that every wasted second might cost dearly.

"First we need to get out of here," Mrs. Shanahan replies coolly. "Then we can look at our options afterward."

It's a fair answer, and Rose doesn't object. Instead,

she turns around in her seat and glances out through the rear window.

The view is distorted by raindrops dancing riotously on the glass. Behind them, the buildings of Oakwood High stand in a dark contrast to the dreary gray sky.

To her eyes, it doesn't look like a school anymore. It looks like an asylum from a horror story, and she has a nagging feeling that she's set foot there for the last time.

This is the final thought going through Rose Lavine's head before a bright light—blue and red at the same time—bursts through the side window to her left.

A second later, the crash comes as the patrol car collides with the rear door of the Kia, sending a barrage of shattered glass in over Kitty and Rose.

Chapter Eleven

Rose screams at the top of her lungs, but the sound of her voice is drowned out by the shrill creaking of the chassis shrinking in on them like a coffin of metal and glass as the car skids sideways across the asphalt.

In front of her—in a moment her brain somehow stretches out in slow motion—she sees Mrs. Shanahan hunched over in the front seat, wedged between the seat and the car's airbag. Her arms look like they're clinging to the big white cushion of air, and her head is turned so Rose can see her face. The eyes are wide open ... but Mrs. Shanahan is *not* conscious, because her hazel brown irises have disappeared behind the eyelids, and white is the only color left.

Now the final bang comes—the one that brings the Kia to a halt because it collides with a lamppost on

Kitty's side. And just as the car stops, so do Rose's thoughts as her head knocks against something, leaving her unconscious.

How long she remains in the deep darkness of her subconscious mind, hanging limply in the seatbelt, she'll never know. But the two things that wake her up she will remember for the rest of her life.

One is the sound of glass shards crunching beneath the feet of the two officers as they approach the wreckage. The second is the intense pain as one of them reaches his arm through the shattered side window, grabs her hair, and starts pulling her out.

He makes three failed attempts with growing ferocity before biting the bullet and snapping open the buckle of her seatbelt. Rose tries to fight him off, but she has no strength, and she's floating in and out of consciousness—and before she knows it, she's halfway out of the broken window.

Shards of glass are still stuck in its rubber frame. She can feel them tearing and cutting their way through her jeans just below her hip and, after that, through the skin.

An explosion of pain hits her neck, sending bolts of lightning through her spine as she lands on the rough surface of the asphalt.

He stands there, leaning over her, *towering* over her. Most of his face is laid in darkness, and her vision is blurred by the raindrops hailing down on her, but she doesn't need more than the murky outline to recognize him.

Officer Mendez. Police assistant. Murderous monster.

"I told you to stay in the gym," he says in a voice that chills Rose's spine. Because he sounds genuinely disappointed—like the parent of a child who has broken a promise—and that only makes him seem even more insane.

"F-fuck you," Rose murmurs, after which she tries to spit on him. However, all she accomplishes is to pour a pink mixture of drool and blood down her own chin.

"Get her into the patrol car," old Sheriff Hodge says behind Mendez. "I'll check to see if the other two are still kicking."

This last sentence hits Rose like a blow to the kidney. Because the last thing she registered before losing consciousness was the collision with the lamppost—and it was right outside Kitty's window when it happened.

She tries to get to her knees so she can look through the side window of the wrecked car, but she only manages to push herself halfway up before Officer Mendez grabs her hair again.

"No more of your brilliant ideas," he says as he

yanks her with him in the direction of the patrol car. "You've done more than enough for today."

She opens her mouth, not really knowing what she's going to say. It doesn't matter, though, because the pain as the open, bleeding wound below her hip meets the rough surface of the asphalt renders her unable to speak.

Behind her sounds a sharp sizzle, like an amplified version of a snake's hiss, and she is struck by an unnerving premonition. A premonition that becomes a certainty the second after as the wet asphalt next to her takes on a faint, orange glare.

"Holy shit!" Sheriff Hodge groans. "Hurry up and get her into the car. I need you here."

Being the good assistant he is, Mendez promptly responds. He speeds up, drags Rose mercilessly over to the patrol car, opens the door, and hurls her in as if she were nothing but a rag doll.

Only now, lying there with her face buried in the back seat, inhaling a scent of cleaning alcohol and leather, does Rose realize there must be two patrol cars. That the two officers must have come in separate ones.

With painful effort, she pushes herself up to a sitting position. She was right, there are two. The one she is sitting in, which is unscathed, and the other one, which they used to torpedo the Kia. That one is *not* unscathed. Most of the front end is bent so far backward that the radiator grille almost touches the windshield.

And it is—*thank God*—also that one that has caught fire.

From the burning patrol car, she turns her gaze to the Kia, where Hodge is struggling to pull out Mrs. Shanahan. She is still unconscious. At least that's what Rose hopes.

Does it even make a difference? They'll kill us anyway.

The thought is her own, but it surprises her like an ambush, and she has to strain not to let it push her over the edge to a breakdown.

She squints her eyes and tries to spot Kitty. She must be in the back seat behind the broken window, knocked out like Mrs. Shanahan, but Rose can't see her. The increasing dark gray smoke from the hood of the patrol car doesn't exactly make the task any easier either.

After several hard—and downright ruthless—jerks, the old sheriff has finally gotten the unconscious teacher pulled all the way out of the vehicle, and he dumps her limp body indifferently onto the asphalt, just as Mendez did to Rose.

Except that Mrs. Shanahan isn't unconscious any-more. Rose is sure she saw her twist her upper body, just slightly, during the fall so she avoided hitting with her face first.

She's planning something, Rose thinks—and when she sees Mrs. Shanahan's hand move slowly out from under her abdomen, she knows it's true. Because that hand clutches the car key. Holds it the same way you would hold a knife.

You have to help her!

With that thought as a driving force, Rose starts banging on the window and kicking wildly at the metal grid between the patrol car's front and rear seats.

"HEY! PIGS!" she screams. It's not sophisticated, but it's the best her brain can come up with right now. "LET ME OUT! I DEMAND THAT YOU LET ME OUT!"

It's working. Hodge walks toward her instead of grabbing Mrs. Shanahan's hair, as he was about to, and Mendez releases the doorknob of the Kia and turns around.

"YOU CAN'T KEEP ME LOCKED UP WITHOUT READING ME MY RIGHTS!" Rose continues, trying to look everywhere but at Mrs. Shanahan, who is now pushing herself up. "IT'S ... IT'S AGAINST THE LAW!"

Now old Sheriff Hodge stops in front of the patrol car's side window and leans down, his face so close to the glass surface that she can see all his deep, furrowed wrinkles and the icy hatred in his ash-gray eyes.

His face is wet from the rain, and water beads trickle down his cheeks like tears, but that doesn't soften the sepulchral expression. Rather the opposite, as they reflect the flames that now have really taken hold of the other patrol car.

For a while, Hodge says nothing. He just stares at her, leaving the monotonous drumming of rain on the roof to fill the soundscape. Then he speaks in a voice that, despite being little more than a whisper, manages to cut clearly through the rain-soaked window.

"Now you listen closely," he says. "It's not a question of whether or not it's going to happen. Because it is. We *will* kill you. We'll kill *all* the deviants. There is nothing you can do about that, no matter how much you stomp on the ground and whine like a baby. *How* it's going to happen, on the other hand ..."

He pauses as he stares at her, as if he is expecting her to take the opportunity to ask clarifying questions.

Rose doesn't ask any questions. She wouldn't be able to even if she wanted. She can't speak. Christ, she can hardly breathe. Besides, the message has sunk in.

Keep pissing me off and your departure from this world will be extremely unpleasant. That is roughly the essence. And she doesn't doubt for a second that the old sheriff means it. After all, she saw with her own eyes what they did to poor *I PAUSED MY GAME TO BE HERE*. A fate like that she wouldn't wish for her worst—

"AAARGH! YOU BITCH! FUCK! FUCKING BITCH!"

Mendez' screams are shrill and full of both pain and surprise—and when Rose leans to the side so she can see past Hodge's hip, she understands why.

Mrs. Shanahan's car key is currently buried in Mendez' shoulder muscle, and the hand he is trying to pull it out with is already red with blood.

The teacher is leaning against the front door of the Kia. She looks dizzy and exhausted. Clearly, the surprise attack cost her almost all her remaining strength. On the upside, though, her hand is holding a new weapon. One that compensates for her fatigue and evens out the odds.

Only now, when she points it at Mendez, does he realize what has happened. That she has been cunning enough to snatch his service weapon while his focus was on the key penetrating the skin of his shoulder.

"Let us go," she groans. "Let the girl out of the car and let us go. This doesn't have to get any worse."

To clarify what she means by those words, Mrs. Shanahan adjusts her aim so that the barrel of the gun points directly at Mendez' chest.

And therein lies her fateful mistake. It should have been directed at Hodge ... who also carries a gun in his belt.

Chapter Twelve

Despite his furrowed face, his crooked fingers with sporadic liver spots, and his old man posture, there is nothing wrong with Sheriff Hodge's motor memory. His hands are quick as lightning, and his aim is true.

The bullet hits the wrist of the hand in which Mrs. Shanahan holds the gun, shattering her pearl bracelet —as well as the bone behind it—into a thousand pieces.

Without a doubt, Hodge could easily have placed that bullet in her heart or her brain instead. But even in her current state of terror, Rose is fully aware of why he didn't.

Keep pissing me off and your departure from this world will be extremely unpleasant.

Whether Mrs. Shanahan grasps it is another matter. In fact, she doesn't seem to grasp anything at this moment. She just stands there, mouth wide open in a silent scream and one hand closed around the other as if she's trying to put it back in place. But no matter how hard she tries, it won't stay put. It has been reduced to a bloody, floppy lump of flesh connected to her forearm only by a thin strand of torn muscle tissue.

Mrs. Shanahan no longer poses a threat. Both officers know this, and neither of them hesitate before walking over, grabbing her arms, and dragging her along.

"Oh God, no," Rose hears herself whimper as she realizes what they're planning to do. "No, don't do that. Please, not that!"

But the two policemen couldn't give a rat's ass about her opinion of what they should or shouldn't do. They keep walking until they've reached the burning patrol car, after which they open its back door and shove Mrs. Shanahan inside. Then they slam the door, which, just like the one Rose is pounding on now, can only be opened from the outside.

The succeeding minute is insufferable. Through a prism-like veil of tears, Rose watches helplessly as flames consume the front seats of the patrol car and then start reaching for Mrs. Shanahan. She hears the teacher's desperate, animalistic screams, which gradually die out and instead turn into an anguished cough.

As excruciating and brutal as it is, Rose still can't look away. Something keeps her gaze fixed on the terrible scenario, forces her to stare at it against her will.

Now the fire grabs a hold of the sleeve of Mrs. Shanahan's jacket, climbs up from there, and reaches her hair. She screams in pain and horror as her long, dark brown locks shrink, curling into a sticky mass that clings to her scalp like black tar. Below, the skin on her face starts to bubble and burst, then melts like wax under the intense heat, while what once was eye makeup turns into eerie, colorful tears of chemical colors on her cheeks.

And that's how it ends. Kristal Shanahan—whose only crime was letting out two girls imprisoned in a high school gym—ends her days in the back seat of a patrol car, engulfed in flames. All while her executioners stand and watch; one with his hands on his hips, the other with his arms crossed. Just like they stood after hanging up the dead boy in the sculpture outside the school. Perfectly calm and unaffected, almost ... proud?

Behind Rose, a faint click sounds as the other back door is opened. For an irrational split second, she's convinced it must be one of the officers who has somehow snuck around behind her, even though she can still see them both standing outside the burning patrol car.

It's not one of the officers. It's Kitty, now squatting outside the door with a finger on her lip and a desperate *not a sound* expression in her eyes.

She looks terrible. Her eye makeup is smeared in two large, dark gray patches on her cheeks. Above these, her bangs are soaked in blood and stick to her forehead.

Now she reaches out her hand. So does Rose—and when their quivering fingers touch, they both struggle not to let their emotions get the better of them.

Knowing that it won't be long before the officers turn their attention back to her, Rose crawls over the seat and out to her childhood friend.

They exchange a look containing all the things they can't say out of fear that the officers will hear them. Then they grab each other's hand again.

And run.

PART TWO

Hemlock Ridge

❧

"Woods are fascinating. The same path can lead you down to a beautiful, sunlit clearing during the daytime and at night drag you down into a terrifying, shadowy crater."

RANDALL MORGAN, *THE FLOOD*

Chapter Thirteen

The handlebars are slightly skewed, one pedal is missing its plate, and the front wheel wobbles with every half spin. Nevertheless, Rose prefers riding this old, rusty bike to Kitty's suggestion that they could try hitchhiking their way to Sebastian's school. That said, she wasn't too proud of herself when they found—and stole—the bike outside the FullCart supermarket downtown.

But worrying about that is of no use. At that point, neither of them were able to run anymore, and stopping was not an option. Thus, they had to find an alternative solution—and since Rose only has two driving lessons on her curriculum vitae, the bike seemed like the sensible choice. Therefore, she is now pedaling

away while Kitty sits on the luggage rack, clinging
to her.

The rain is pouring down on them without pause,
they're both drenched and freezing, and her legs still
hurt ... but of all Rose's worries right now, these are the
least. Before them come the officers—and before them
comes Sebastian.

Eleven missed calls. Eleven!

Fortunately, they haven't seen any trace of their
pursuers. Not since they escaped while they were busy
burning Mrs. Shanahan like a witch at the stake.

For a brief second, that image rematerializes on
Rose's retinas—Mrs. Shanahan's lips forming the last,
soundless scream as the skin on her cheeks melts away
—and she almost loses control of the bike.

"Whoa, what the hell, Red?" Kitty exclaims behind
her back.

"I'm sorry," Rose replies. "I'm ... a bit off. A little
shaken."

Kitty responds by placing her cheek against Rose's
back and tightening her grip around her.

"We got away from them," she says. "That's what
matters."

"Yeah, but what they did to Mrs. Shanahan ..."

"That's *all* that matters," Kitty repeats, this time in
a sharper, almost reprimanding tone. Underneath it,
however, lies a frailty that tells Rose that her friend is

just as shaken as her but tries to toughen up for her sake ... and for that Rose is grateful.

A few hundred yards ahead, Coulton's town sign appears on the side of the road. A cobalt blue sign with gold lettering, which seems far too pompous, bordering on the ridiculous, when you know the humble size of the town. The fact that the sign has been put up in front of the first row of trees in the Hemlock Ridge Forest, all somewhat withered and in dire need of a trimming, doesn't exactly help with the overall impression either.

Nonetheless, the sight of the sign should be a relief for Rose. After all, Coulton is her hometown. But for some reason, it only makes her more anxious.

Maybe it's because it indicates that the goal is just around the corner, so she will get some answers soon about what has happened to her little brother.

As if she's read her mind, Kitty tightens her grip once more and says:

"We're almost there, and I'm sure Sebastian is fine. Just you wait and see."

Rose nods but doesn't say anything.

Two minutes later, she steps on the brakes, causing the bike to lose speed. It's not that they've reached the finish line. For that, they still need to cross the inter-section at the end of the current neighborhood and then turn left.

No, Rose slows down because she spots someone she knows—and because she's shocked by what they're doing.

Denise Cumberland is one of her mom's close friends, and she is also an assistant to Rose's regular dentist. So, Rose knows Denise quite well—and if anyone were to ask her to describe her, she would use words like *sensible, confident, kind but firm* ... and maybe a bit *snobby*.

For the same reason, what Denise is doing makes no sense. Because Denise is hanging up laundry. It's pouring down rain, and she's out in her yard—wearing pajamas, mind you—putting laundry on the clothesline.

Now she spots them and raises her hand in a greeting as if it's completely normal to see her friend's daughter rolling through the neighborhood during school hours with a passenger on the back of her bike.

Rose hesitantly lifts her hand from the handlebars and waves back. As she does so, she makes eye contact with Denise. It only lasts a second or two, but it's enough to draw the parallel. Enough to identify the clear resemblance between Denise's eyes and her mom's eyes this morning.

The blankness in them. *The absence* in them.

With that discovery comes a contemplation that

has her shuddering: How many have been affected by this? Is it even possible to escape from it?

She shakes her head to push away her thoughts, then fixes her gaze on the center lines of the road and starts pedaling harder.

For a while it works. For a while, she can keep the fear and the disturbing thoughts in the background by locking her gaze on the road and focusing on moving forward.

But then she turns onto Anvil Lane, and her gaze falls upon Pine Hill Middle School.

And the flashing lights of the two ambulances parked outside it.

Chapter Fourteen

"I'm serious, Red. It's a really bad idea."

Kitty is probably right ... no, Kitty is *undoubtedly* right. It *is* a bad idea, but Rose has no choice. Every cell in her body agreed when they convinced her to get off the bike—and they're also agreeing now, moving her feet in the direction of the vehicles in front of the school.

"You don't have to come with me," she says, gesturing back toward the bike she left outside the half-wall at the gate leading to the school. "You can take the bike. I don't mind."

"As if," Kitty says, a bit irritably but not outright angrily. "I'm going with you, but it's *in, get him,* and then *out,* got it?"

Rose doesn't answer, and she also only partially

listens. Because now she has spotted the three additional vehicles in the schoolyard next to the ambulances.

Two of them are military trucks of the type used to transport groups of soldiers. The last is a medium-sized school bus whose rain-speckled windows frame the silhouettes of the kids already occupying its seats.

At the door of the bus are two men in white coats, and in front of these is a line of children, crammed together like cattle for the slaughter and held in check by armed soldiers.

The context is as clear as it is horrifying. Because a single glance at their faces is enough to tell Rose that these children aren't stuck in the same apathetic state that her mom and the students at her school were.

They are aware of what is going on and they are terrified.

"I don't see him," she groans, and then again, a little louder, "Oh God, Kitty, I don't see Sebastian anywhere."

"Take it easy, maybe ..." Kitty begins, but she never finishes the sentence. She just makes a labored swallowing motion and looks down at the ground.

Now, two more children get on the bus after a brief examination by one of the doctors while the other signals one of the soldiers to bring him the next couple.

There is something wrong with the soldiers, just

like there was with Hodge and Mendez. Rose doesn't doubt that for a second. They have the same glow in their eye that they had. As though they are struggling to contain their amusement behind their stern exterior. One of them in particular scares her. It's the way he is standing with his forearm resting on a machine gun hanging in a strap over his shoulder. The way his index finger is tapping impatiently on its barrel.

As if he has felt her gaze resting on him, this soldier turns his head and looks at Rose.

With a shaking hand, she gently grabs Kitty's elbow and leads her back toward the gate. She continues to back away until, after what feels like an eternity, the soldier finally turns his attention back toward the line. Then she changes direction and drags Kitty along the half-wall toward the parking lot next to the school.

"What are you doing?"

"We're never gonna get past them," Rose replies. "But I saw Principal Holmes walk out into the parking lot. If anyone has a chance of stopping them, it has got to be him."

"Homie? But what if he's also ... you know, zombiefied?"

"We've got to try."

Francis Holmes, or *Principal Homie* as the kids liked to call him when Rose and Kitty went to Pine Hill, was pretty popular among the students. He had just the right combination of kindness and authority that a school principal should have. Even in hectic situations —like when one of the students in Rose's class brought a knife to school and threatened another kid —you could always count on Principal Holmes to stay calm and get things under control. Because once Homie took off his glasses and aimed his brown lie detector eyes at a potential perpetrator, the truth always came out.

In light of this, it hits Rose like a punch to the gut to see him now. Seeing the wisdom in those eyes replaced by emptiness as he lifts his gaze from the car key in his hand and catches sight of them.

"Rose Lavine and Katherine Burns?" he says in a voice so gravelly you'd think he'd spent the whole morning throwing down shots at a bar. "What are you doing here?"

"Hi, Principal Holmes. We, um ... we came to get my little brother, Sebastian, but right now we need your help."

"I see. For what?"

For a moment, Rose is left speechless by the absurdity of that question, because from where he stands right now, it's impossible that he can't see what's going on in the schoolyard behind them.

"To stop that!" Kitty says, pointing in the direction

of the bus. "They're planning to do something to the kids. To *your students*!"

He glances over there but not for more than a split second before shifting his attention back to Kitty and Rose.

"It's just part of a random check," he says. "We were notified this morning. They're only here to check that they're not sick. In some places in Pennsylvania and Maryland, they've had to shut down schools completely because of some new virus affecting children. That's what they're trying to prevent here."

"A virus?" Rose scoffs without making the slightest attempt to hide her simmering anger. Not that she'd expect him to even register it. "Then why did they put them on the bus?"

A pause. So long that Rose and Kitty exchange a worried look. Then their old principal suddenly shrugs his shoulders and says:

"They're the experts. I think they know what they're doing. Don't you?"

Rose takes a breath and opens her mouth, preparing to express her indignation, but she doesn't have time to say anything before she's interrupted by a sound coming from the schoolyard. The sound of a hydraulic brake being released, followed by an engine gassing up.

"It's leaving!" Kitty cries. "The bus is leaving, Rose. What do we do?"

Rose offers her no answer because she is already well on her way over to the half-wall surrounding the school, hoping she'll be able to see through the windows of the bus as it rolls by out on the street.

She is—and this time the light hits the windows from a different angle, so she can see more than just dark silhouettes of schoolchildren.

So she can see their frightened faces.

And among them is his.

Chapter Fifteen

Rose Lavine's actions in the succeeding minutes aren't rational. She is driven by a mixture of instinct, panic, rage, and powerlessness that is as potent as it is dangerous.

Had there been time to think it through, she might have adjusted a few details. But the bus is leaving, and she doesn't have time. Therefore, she sprints straight to her old school principal, rips the car key out of his hand, and then proceeds to the black Audi that she knows belongs to him.

She gets in, locks the doors, and tells herself she won't open them, no matter how much he bangs on the window and yells at her.

But Principal Holmes doesn't follow her. He remains standing in the parking lot, staring down at his empty hand in bewilderment. Kitty, on the other hand, is right on Rose's heels, and now she starts knocking frantically on the window of the passenger side.

"Let me in, Red!"

Rose puts the key into the ignition, turns it, and keeps her eyes directed straight ahead while placing both hands on the steering wheel. Then she changes her mind and unlocks the door.

"Hurry up," she says. "And buckle up. I don't know what I'm doing."

"How many driving lessons have you—"

"Two," Rose interrupts, after which she steps on the gas pedal and sends the car off in an uneven curve across the parking lot.

Kitty's answer comes in the form of a pair of wide-open eyes and a click from her throat as she swallows.

"I drove a bit with my mom too," Rose adds, attempting to offer her friend some reassurance. However, considering that one of the rims scrape against the curb a second later, it probably doesn't work too well.

The road outside of the school is scattered with large puddles of water, and despite her efforts to avoid them, Rose hits a few, causing the Audi to lose traction momentarily before regaining its grip on the road surface.

She ought to slow down, she is well aware of that.

But the bus is already at the intersection of Killburn Street and Shepherds Lane. And once it's out of sight, they won't stand a chance.

She bites her lower lip, squints her eyes, and tries to recall everything she's learned about the art of driving.

Ten and two is the only thing that pops into her head, and she's already got that covered. Her hands sit where they're supposed to on the steering wheel.

At least it's an automatic transmission. Otherwise, they wouldn't have gotten far.

"You're a bit close to the curb," Kitty says. She speaks gently, but her edginess still shines through.

"I'm sorry, Kitty," Rose says, correcting the course. "I'm doing my best."

"I know. They're turning."

Rose follows the invisible line from Kitty's fingertip out through the rain-spattered windshield to the traffic lights. Sure enough, the front end of the bus has already vanished behind a building on Killburn Street.

Rose feels her pulse rise in her temples—and as it rises, so does the speed of the car. She gets ready to turn when she reaches the intersection.

"What the hell is *that?*" she hears Kitty whisper out between clenched teeth.

For a moment, Rose has no idea what she's talking about. Then she discovers that Kitty's gaze is directed upward. In the direction of the last lamppost before the traffic lights.

In it hangs a man. A *dead* man. His face is dark purple and swollen, his clothes torn to pieces, as if he has been dragged across the ground.

The sight shocks Rose, paralyzes her so she almost forgets that she has to turn at the traffic lights—and when she realizes, she jerks the steering wheel so hard that the rear end skids sideways. It hits a plastic container at the curb, sending a cascade of trash out on the road.

"Christ, Red! You've got to be careful!"

"I know, I know. Sorry."

For the next minute or so, the bus stays on Killburn Street, and Rose gradually catches up with it while the foggy contours of shops and homes flicker by outside the Audi's rain-soaked windows.

The bus is driving fast. Much faster than Rose likes to drive. And it's not just because of her lack of experience behind the wheel. There are also the slippery roads and poor visibility caused by the rain to consider. Not to mention the fact that the bus is jam-packed with scared kids.

This final thought gives her the courage to press the accelerator down the last bit, making it touch the floor.

The Audi's growl turns into a roar, and she feels a

rush in her stomach as they are pulled forward. It feels like sitting on a roller coaster in an amusement park ... but not one of the fun ones. One that she has been forced to ride against her will.

At least it's working. The rear of the bus is getting closer and closer. In a minute she can overtake it, and then hopefully she can get it to—

"HE'S BRAKING! WATCH OUT!"

In the wake of Kitty's warning cry follows a series of events that Rose only records in fragments. She sees the bus' blurry taillights flare up and become huge behind the wet windshield. They resemble the eyes of a monster in a fantasy story, red and menacing. At the same time, Kitty's hand comes flying into her field of vision. It grabs the steering wheel, pulls it, and forces the Audi to turn sharply to the right.

Almost immediately after, a piercing crack sounds as Rose's side mirror collides with the rear of the bus and breaks off, after which the car continues onto the pavement. Here it's brought to a halt by a wooden fence while the bus rolls on down the street as if nothing has happened.

Rose could have given up at that moment. Accepted her defeat and consoled herself with the fact that she at least made a brave attempt.

She might even have done just that ... if she hadn't caught another glimpse of her little brother. But she did—and this time he spotted her as well. She knows he did because she saw him banging on the back window, shaping her name with his lips.

Without hesitation, she throws the Audi into reverse and drives in an arc backward until she is back on the road. Then she resumes the hunt for the bus, which once more has been reduced to a blurry, yellow square somewhere far ahead in the rain.

Soon it will be all the way out of town, and that means woodland, rolling terrain, and hairpin turns. All of which will make her task harder.

"Hold on," she says, looking over at Kitty, halfway expecting to be met with protests.

Kitty doesn't protest. She simply gives her a solemn nod, then grabs the roof handle with one hand and pushes the other against the dashboard.

"Let's get that asshole," she then says.

Chapter Sixteen

According to the watch on Rose's wrist, it's still day-time, but it doesn't feel that way anymore. For on this October day, when the rain falls in heavy drops and envelops the car in a blanket of mist, it's darkness that reigns in the wooded area outside Coulton.

Everything around them feels perilous. The road winds beneath them, treacherous and smooth like a black snake, and the branches of the thick foliage whisper as they are rustled by the breeze. Dire warnings to anyone daring to venture into their domain.

The windshield wipers don't exactly lift the spirit inside the car either. The constant scratching as they slide from side to side makes Rose's skin crawl.

"There has got to be a straight stretch soon," Kitty says next to her. "It can't all be turns and hills, can it?"

Rose shrugs, not moving her gaze from the road. Or from the two little dots of red light out there. She's afraid that it all could be over in a heartbeat if she does.

Even when the headlight is reflected in a pair of eyes at the edge of the ditch—probably a fox or a rabbit —she doesn't let herself be distracted.

Whatever the cost, she's going to catch up with that bus.

A few minutes later, she gets the best chance so far as the bus slows down and turns onto a side road. Rose grabs the opportunity to significantly reduce the distance between them.

"Wait a minute," Kitty exclaims as they follow the bus onto the side road. "I know this place. This is where we camped with the Scouts when I was little. We went swimming in Haywood here."

"The river?"

Kitty nods and then lets out a small gasp as if she's remembered something important. She raises her hand and points out the windshield.

"This is our chance. There's a straight patch around here where they'll have to slow down because there's a bridge over the river. It's ... after that hill right there, I think."

Sure enough, once Rose reaches the top of the hill and can look past it, she sees the bus driving on a straight patch of road, stretching so far that she can only make out the contours of the bridge in the distance.

She repeats her message to Kitty from earlier—*hold on*—with a look. Next, she tightens her grip on the steering wheel and steps on the gas.

Yard by yard, the distance grows smaller until she is right behind the bus again. This time, however, she's not going to give it the chance to hit the brakes right in front of her. So, she pulls out in the left lane.

Her plan is to pass it before they reach the bridge, where the road narrows to a single lane. That way, she'll be able to cut off the bus and block the road so it has to stop.

That is the plan. It could have worked ... if the driver of the bus had allowed her to pass.

He doesn't. Instead, he pulls over in her lane.

The metal screams as the two vehicles collide, and so do the two girls. They scream in pure, unison horror while the narrow country road becomes the arena for an unjust gladiator fight between the two machines.

Rose jerks at the steering wheel and steps on the brake—*stomps* on it—but it's in vain. Principal Holmes' Audi no longer takes its orders from her. It only follows the commands it receives from the slippery asphalt and the wet autumn leaves that the trees have cast aside.

And right now, they're telling it to steer directly toward the metal railing on the bridge's left side—and that it needs to maintain that course, no matter how much Rose pulls the wheel.

Now the underside of the Audi hits the slanted part at the beginning of the railing, and the cabin is filled with a dissonant, metallic squeal as the car is lifted and tilted upside-down.

In the ensuing, weightless seconds, it's as if time slows down for Rose. As if the shock and adrenaline enable her to pick up details that she shouldn't have been able to capture.

She sees Kitty in the passenger seat, frantically reaching for nothing, while the glass in the side window behind her shatters, and the view behind her changes from the dark trees of the forest to the gray clouds of the sky and subsequently to the ominous surface of the Haywood River.

And because she, in this strange, weightless moment, is able to see what will happen when the vehicle hits the water, Rose tries to reach for her friend.

In vain. The collision with the water's surface does exactly what her instinct told her it would. It tosses Kitty's upper body helplessly to the side so that her exposed neck meets the shards of glass in the frame of the window.

A blood-red necklace emerges across Kitty's neck

and then mixes with the floodwater rushing in through the window behind her. That's the last thing Rose sees before she's overwhelmed by the freezing cold of the water and pulled into a chaotic, suffocating darkness where her reality is reduced to a series of fleeting flashes that shoot forth, lighting up her field of vision the way a lightning strike can briefly light up the sky during a storm.

The first flash is down in the darkness under the water, where she sees her own hands, illuminated only by the dim glow from the dashboard, as they fumble desperately with the buckle of the seatbelt.

The second flash is a dazzling, orange-colored light as something catches fire somewhere above the surface of the water. It's the school bus, it must be, but she can't confirm it because the callous hands of the water keep pulling her in the opposite direction.

The third flash reveals treetops sloping over her from both sides as she is swirled helplessly around by the current, alternately coughing out water and gasping for breath.

The fourth—and final—flash is nothing more than the outline of bubbles in front of her face as the last remnant of oxygen is pulled from her lungs.

After that, only darkness and cold remain. They envelop her, tightening their embrace until she no longer has the strength or the will to fight back.

Chapter Seventeen

The sound of the bright voice reaches her but only as something peripheral. Like a fragile ember flaring up in a pile of ashes to then die out again immediately.

And why should she bother reacting to it? It's not real. None of this is real. It's a dream. A velvet-black labyrinth filled with the echoes of distant birds chirping and trickling water. A maze without worries, without fear … and without end. She could wander around here forever and never have to—

"Rose!" the voice repeats. "Wake up, Rose!"

No, she refuses. She doesn't want to go back. She doesn't want to wake up, because she … she … what?

"ROSE, FOR GOD'S SAKE! WAKE UP!" reverberates through the corridors of the maze, and suddenly, like rays of sunlight penetrating a heavy cover of clouds, light breaks through the walls. It blinds her, scorches her retinas, while the silhouette of the voice's owner gradually manifests.

Sebastian. He is kneeling in front of her. His face is pale, his hair is damp and clings to his forehead, raindrops are dripping from the tip of his nose, and his eyes are wet with tears. But he's smiling.

She opens her mouth to ask what has happened but is instantly overwhelmed by the sensation of suffocation. She gasps for breath but instead feels her mouth and throat fill with muddy water.

She rolls over on her side, coughing, gurgling, gasping, and vomiting uncontrollably, again and again, until her lungs are finally able to take in a bit of oxygen.

"Careful," Sebastian says, placing a hand gently on her shoulder. "You were in the water for a long time. I tried to get you out, but the current kept pulling you away."

For a moment, those words make no sense at all to Rose. Then her gaze slides to the side, along the riverbank on which she is lying, and the whole thing comes crashing down on her like a new wave. A flood that tries to drown her, only in pain and sorrow rather than water.

The officers, the gym, Mrs. Shanahan in the burning patrol car, the bus, the bridge and ... *oh God.*

"K-Kitty?" she sobs and looks up at Sebastian, who, with pursed lips and a tormented expression on his face, shakes his head slowly from side to side.

"She ... didn't make it," he says, raising his hand to his neck as if he somehow knows what happened to Kitty and is about to illustrate it with a gesture. In the end, though, he only scratches his chin and then lets his hand fall into his lap. "She's dead, Rose. I ... I'm so sorry."

Rose knows it's the truth. Hell, she witnessed it firsthand. Still, she closes her eyes and shakes her head fiercely, as if hoping she can magically change it, if only her will is strong enough.

When she opens her eyes again, nothing has changed. She's still lying on the riverbank's rough bed of sandy soil, pebbles, leaves, and branches, all of it as cold, wet, and sticky as her.

And she is still responsible for the death of her best friend.

"We need to get out of here," Sebastian says. "The bus, it ... it caught fire after it crashed up on the bridge and it was complete mayhem, so I don't think they noticed that I got away. But if they come looking for us, they'll probably be following the river."

He raises his hand and points, but Rose doesn't look in that direction. She looks at *him* for a moment, in silence, and then she suddenly reaches out her hands, grabs him, and pulls him in.

"You're okay?" she whispers, burying her face in his shoulder.

"I'm alright, Sis," he confirms in a voice as shaky and muddy as hers. "I'm alright."

For a while, Rose stays like that, her arms around her little brother and her fingers clutching the fabric of his jacket. Then she takes a deep breath, pulls herself together, and forces her fingers to let go of him. Because it's not over yet, and she's the oldest. It's her job to take care of him, not the other way around. And right now, that job involves pushing her grief, guilt, shame, and pain into the background.

She holds out her hand and gestures for him to help her get up. Once he has done so, she nods in the direction of the forest.

"We'll go in there so we're harder to spot, but not too far from the river. It's the only landmark we have."

Sebastian nods, but it doesn't look like he's listening very closely. His gaze keeps wandering down to her leg.

Now she looks down there too—and sighs loudly. Truth be told, it's more out of surprise than actual pain, as her body is still pretty numb from the cold water, so it doesn't hurt yet. It will, though, because the wood splinter is buried at least two inches in her thigh muscle.

"Give me a break," she sighs, after which she gently presses with her fingertips, first on the dark red stain on her jeans below the wound and then on the side of the wooden splinter itself.

And yes, she isn't completely numb to the pain, after all.

"You have to leave it in," Sebastian says. "I saw a video on YouTube about it. It was a doctor talking about the *Last of Us* series, and he said Joel would have been dead when he pulled out that metal rod in one of the last episodes. You have to leave it there so you don't get infected or lose too much blood, and then go to the emergency room."

And how much help do you think I'll get in a hospital right now? Rose thinks, but she keeps it to herself, and she also takes her little brother's advice and leaves the wooden stump in place.

The sound of rustling leaves—far away, but not *that* far away—makes them both jolt and glance back along the river.

"If you can walk, I really think—"

"Yeah, we need to move away from the river," Rose

says, after which she puts her arm on his shoulder so she can lean on him.

Then the two siblings leave the riverbank and wander into the shadows beneath the dark trees of the Hemlock Ridge Forest.

Chapter Eighteen

It's a quarter to five in the afternoon when Rose finally admits defeat and accepts the bitter truth.

They're lost. At some point, they accidentally lost their orientation and moved too far away from the river. And they were so careful. They walked parallel to it while trying to keep the sound of the running water within earshot.

They have not been able to hear it for over an hour now.

Raindrops bouncing off the leaves of trees. Branches rustling in the breeze. A maddening choir of buzzing mosquitoes. A screeching crow. A plane humming in the distance.

All of that, yes. But no trickling of water. No river.

"Is it still helping?" Sebastian asks. He is climbing a moss-covered slope some distance ahead of her.

"Yeah, it's great," Rose replies, raising her walking cane demonstratively a few inches off the ground. "And it makes me look pretty badass, doesn't it?"

Sebastian rolls his eyes but still smiles.

In reality, the cane is nothing more than a thick stick of about five feet that he found on the forest floor and gave to her when the splinter in her thigh really started to hurt. And she has to hand it to him that, for lack of better, it's an excellent crutch.

Now, if he could just find bug spray.

The mosquitoes are driving her nuts. Those tiny, blood-sucking bastards hang in a cloud around her head, whirring like miniature helicopters next to her ears.

And yes, she does realize that there's a deeper reason why they're making her so furious. That it's really about her being on the verge of a nervous breakdown.

Because the world has lost its mind. Because she misses her mom, whom she is no longer sure she will ever get back. Because her best friend is dead. Because she is afraid that Sebastian and herself might be heading for the same fate. Because they're lost in the county's largest forest while the day gradually draws to a close—and because she absolutely doesn't feel like spending the night out here.

The idea alone is enough to give her the jitters. Having to sleep on the clammy leaves of the forest floor, which undoubtedly houses thousands of small creepy crawlers.

"Do you see anything?" she shouts to Sebastian, who has just reached the top of the slope.

"Trees," he replies dryly. "Lots of them."

"You're so funny," Rose says just as dryly ... while on the inside she prays that this is indeed what his words are: A poor attempt at being funny.

But Sebastian neither laughs nor smiles when their gazes meet. He looks resigned.

As an eerie extension of this thought, he now sits down, pulls his knees up to his chest, and puts his elbows on top of them. Then he buries his face in his hands.

Small, sparking jolts of pain emerge in her injured thigh as Rose speeds up, but she powers through it and keeps going. Her only moment of hesitation comes as she begins the ascent on the moss-covered slope and her head is filled with a heavy, suffocating fever heat.

Stubbornness and self-control carry her up there, but as soon as she reaches the finish line, they let go and let her fall. She tumbles limply down onto the damp ground next to Sebastian, then halfway crashes, halfway leans in against the tree stump he's sitting in front of.

She wants to comfort him, but she's too out of breath to talk, so she settles for stroking a hand over his back.

"We don't stand a chance," he mutters in a voice that makes him sound twenty years older than he is.

Rose pulls in a few agonizing breaths. Then she gives him a sibling nudge and says:

"Stop whining. It's just a forest. If we don't find the river, we'll find something else to help us get out. A trail or something."

"It's not just the forest I'm talking about," he says. "It's all of it. Even if we do get out, there's no one to help us. Everyone has gone crazy."

"Not everyone," Rose corrects. "We're still normal. So was that teacher I told you about, Mrs. Shanahan. And ... and Kitty, she was also ... sane."

Until you killed her.

"But most aren't. They're like Mom, aren't they?"

Sebastian's question feels like a slap in the face. More than anything because another tone hides beneath the accusatory one. A tone that reveals that he is hoping his big sister will correct him once more. That she will tell him that she spoke to their mom, and it turned out that she is doing just fine.

Rose would have given anything to be able to say that.

"Yeah," is the truth she gives him instead. "Most people I've seen out there are like Mom."

Sebastian doesn't answer, but under her hand she can feel his back tremble as he sighs.

She doesn't say anything either. She just leans all the way back, rests the back of her head against the tree stump, and looks up.

The sky—what little part of it she can make out in a gap between the gloomy carpet of the treetops—is still gray. From it, large raindrops fall on her face, but she can hardly feel them anymore since the cold has penetrated all layers of her clothes as well as her skin.

At least the trees shield them from the wind that she can hear up there.

She closes her eyes and listens to it. How it rustles the leaves as it rises and falls, rises and falls. How it hisses.

Something touches her neck. Sebastian? No, her hand is still resting on his back, and he's in the same stooped position as before, so it can't—

Now it's there again; a sliding motion on her shoulder. It's heavier this time. As if someone has just dumped a rope on her neck and is now slowly pulling it away again.

All of a sudden, the realization hits her, and all her

thoughts disappear in a white explosion of disgust and horror. She jumps up, moves her hand behind her neck, grabs the snake, and throws it away.

It hits the ground six or seven feet down the moss-covered slope and rolls a few more before coming to a halt between a broken branch and some loose rocks. A thick, black snake with a nasty pattern of thin, egg-white lines across its back.

"What's going on?" Sebastian exclaims next to her, but Rose doesn't answer. She simply stares at the snake as it regains control and slithers sideways over the slope until it disappears into a pile of wet, slimy autumn leaves.

She can see it down there, several yards away, and yet she can still feel it. Feel it creep over her neck like some bizarre version of phantom pain.

"Rose," Sebastian says, grabbing her arm, which causes her to jolt again. "Rose, your leg."

For a moment she stays put, her gaze wandering nervously back and forth between Sebastian and the pile of leaves where the legless nightmare creature disappeared. Then the words slowly start to get through to her, and she glances down at her leg.

"Shit."

This one word is the only one she can get across her lips, but it also feels fitting. Because this is a shitty situation, to say the least.

The wood splinter in her thigh has moved, probably when she jumped up, and what used to be a brownish smudge of coagulated blood on her jeans has turned into a shiny, crimson stream of fresh blood trickling down her shin.

It's her imagination—it has to be—but she can almost physically feel her nearly depleted stock of strength seep out of her body along with the red fluid. Feel how dizziness takes its place.

She grabs her jacket, fumbles with it, trying to pull it off so she has something to stop the bleeding with, but it's soaked and has a mind of its own. It clings to her like an extra layer of skin.

"Let me help you," Sebastian says, after which he, without waiting for an answer, pushes her hand away and grabs the sleeve of her jacket.

He's doing much better, so she lets him take over ... even if it's still in there. The little voice in the back of her head telling her that she's failing her responsibilities. That *she* is the oldest.

Once the jacket is off, he points to the tree stump. She nods and leans against it, then turns her leg toward him.

With a calm that both surprises and impresses her, Sebastian wraps the sleeves of the jacket around her thigh and ties them together.

It stings—so much so that her eyes water, and her

teeth involuntarily grind against each other—but it works as intended. The red stream gets weaker and weaker, then stops completely.

"It's not perfect," he says, double-checking the quality of his work. "But it's the best we can do right now. And then we'll just have to share my jacket."

Rose stares at him in amazement. She hadn't even gotten half as far in her considerations. He's right, though. Without her jacket, she will be even more vulnerable to the cold, so sharing his makes perfect sense.

"Who are you and what have you done to my little brother?"

Sebastian shrugs.

"Maybe I'm just not as useless as you like to think."

His smile suggests that he's only joking, yet Rose feels a dab of remorse. Because there is an element of truth in it.

"T-thank you," she stutters.

He makes a sweeping motion as if to say *oh, come on*, but she grabs his hand in the movement and gives it a squeeze.

"I'm serious, Sebastian. You've saved me twice now, and you ... you're *not* useless, okay? You never were."

He stares at her for a while and then nods.

"I think you need to sit down a bit before we move on. You look pretty pale."

Rose looks down at the ground. At the soggy, dark brown forest floor, which is broken only by stones, small branches, and islands of withered leaves.

Wet, sticky fall leaves—like the ones the disgusting snake disappeared under.

"I think I can manage to walk a bit further," she says.

Chapter Nineteen

Do those cursed little fuckers never take a break? Don't they ever need a rest after a hard day's buzzing and whirring and stabbing and sucking and spreading all kinds of diseases? Or are they running shifts that Rose just isn't clever enough to pick up on? Do they check in and out of work all the time without her noticing?

No, she doesn't think so. It doesn't feel that way. It feels *personal*. As if it's the same dark cloud that has been taunting her all afternoon and evening. The same gang of mosquitoes swarming around her in time with the gloomy thoughts whipping around inside her head.

She lifts her gaze from her sneakers, which have now taken on a slight bluish shade because the moon is taking over the job as a light source—which it could do a lot better in her opinion, but let's not go there—and ... and what? Why was it she looked up? What did she want?

Sebastian. Oh, yeah. She wanted to ask Sebastian if he thinks mosquitoes work shifts, but now she can't spot him.

"Sebastian?" she asks out into the semi-darkness of the forest.

"I'm here."

She squints her eyes and looks in the direction of the sound. Yeah, she can make out his silhouette among the trees further on, but it seems fickle. Like a mirage.

"Why are you squatting?"

"What do you mean? I'm making the shelter, remember?"

He pauses, and when Rose still hasn't responded after a while, he adds:

"Christ, Rose. You helped me gather sticks for it."

"Oh ... oh, yeah, of course," she replies, though it doesn't really ring a bell.

It's the fever, she explains to herself. *You're confused because you have a fever. Because of your leg.*

Next to her ears, the buzzing of the mosquitoes grows louder, as if someone has turned a volume knob, and she feels the anger stirring again. Because the wound on her thigh may be the main cause, but she's convinced that the mosquitoes are making it worse. That they also carry the fever poison and seize every opportunity to pump it into her veins.

The only bright spot is that it isn't raining anymore. At least not from the clouds. Sporadic drops still fall every now and then from the wet leaves in the treetops, though. Once in a while, they'll have her twitching because they hit the ground behind her with a sound that could well be mistaken for footsteps.

"That's as good as it gets," Sebastian says, after which he stands up and walks toward her. "We won't get a fire, though, because it's all drenched. Not that I would know how to get it going without a lighter anyway."

He's feeling down. Beaten. That's obvious to Rose, even despite her fever-numbed brain.

"I think it looks great," she says, having gotten close enough to see the results of his work. "You're a natural."

She realizes that she may be sounding a little *too* excited, but she really is quite impressed. Sebastian has managed to build an actual shelter with a pitched roof made of branches and leaves, as well as a sleeping mat made of moss, soil, and something that looks like a cross between reeds and grass.

"What matters is that we have shelter if it starts raining again," he says.

Rose smiles and nods, although she's not sure it's going to make any real difference. At least not tonight, given that she's still so soaked and cold that her teeth are constantly chattering. Moreover, ever since the sun began to set, she has been able to feel the temperature dropping. It causes her skin to contract, making it feel as if she no longer fits in it.

Like the trees, she thinks—without quite knowing what that's supposed to mean.

Then again. Somewhere on the fringes of her consciousness, she does know. Because during the past hour, when twilight has come and the fever has increased, she has had the feeling that the forest is closing in on her. As if the trees are gradually moving closer and closer.

When she has reached the shelter, she drops to her hands and knees and crawls under the primitive roof. There isn't much space, and it makes her a bit claustrophobic, but it is still preferable to sleeping in the open air.

"I'm so hungry," Sebastian says as he creeps in and sits down next to her. "My stomach hurts. Does yours hurt too?"

"We'll find something to eat tomorrow."

This short answer causes Sebastian to squint and stare at her. For a moment, she fears that he might ask her to elaborate. Ask her to present the long list of edible forest berries and mushrooms that she apparently possesses.

Fortunately, he doesn't ask about it. Because there are only two things on that list—*blackberries and blueberries*—and Rose isn't even sure she'd dare to wager on the latter if they found a bush. Because her plant-savvy mom once told her that belladonnas can look like blueberries—and belladonnas are extremely poisonous.

As if he has somehow picked up who she is thinking of, Sebastian catches her gaze and says:

"Do you think Mom and the others will be okay?"

"Well, um ... yeah, of course."

Damnit. She hesitated too long. On the other hand, she is pretty sure that the question was rhetorical and that Sebastian has the same troubling but awfully strong feeling as her. The feeling that *nothing* will ever be the same again—including their mom.

"I, um ... I called her," he says in a voice as fragile as glass. "Before the soldiers took our phones, I tried to call you, but I couldn't get through. So at one point I tried Mom instead."

"Did she answer?"

Sebastian nods and makes a strained swallowing motion.

"I told her there were soldiers kidnapping kids at the school, but it was like she wasn't listening at all.

She kept saying that it was probably just a drill, like when they test the fire alarm. I couldn't get her to listen at all."

Rose isn't surprised. She saw several of her schoolmates staring at a dead teenager in the iron sculpture outside the school as if nothing had happened, and she saw her mom's friend hanging up the laundry in the pouring rain. And those are just a few examples among several others on this fucked-up day where everybody seems to have become completely indifferent to everything.

Hardly has she had these thoughts before a new one pops up in the back of her mind.

The officers weren't indifferent—and neither were the soldiers.

"What did they want with you?" she asks. "The doctors and the soldiers, I mean. Why did they put you on the bus?"

Sebastian shrugs but then gets a thoughtful expression on his face.

"They didn't say very much," he says. "But when the first doctors came into the classrooms this morning, they gave us a paper with some questions. That was before they started putting us on the buses."

"What kind of questions?"

"Like ... puberty stuff, I guess."

"Puberty stuff?"

"Yeah, if we had felt changes on our bodies, if our voices had gotten deeper, if the girls had had their period. Stuff like that."

"What in the world would they need ..." Rose begins, but halfway through the sentence, she interrupts herself with another question: "Was there anyone who wasn't sent to the bus?"

Sebastian replies with a nod.

"There was a group that was going somewhere else. Pete said they gathered them in the gym while the rest of us went to the buses. I don't know if that's true."

Rose feels a new freezing sensation creeping over her skin, but this time it's not triggered by the fever. It's the disturbing feeling that she knows what happened down in that gym. That it's probably something along the lines of what Mendez had originally planned for her and Kitty. However, she doesn't intend to present this theory to her younger brother. His day has been bad enough as it is. No need to sprinkle salt in that wound.

"We'd better try to get some sleep," she says instead, moving closer to him and putting her arm around his shoulders. "I bet things will look brighter tomorrow."

What a load of crap. She knows it, and so does Sebastian ... but he lets it slide and settles for a nod, after which he leans in toward her, just like he used to do when they were little and their mom read stories to them at night.

"Goodnight, Sis."

"Goodnight, Sebastian."

After those words, the silence returns and falls upon brother and sister like a heavy blanket.

The silence isn't absolute, though, because as Rose lies there trying to fall asleep, the fever regains its voice.

And it whispers to her. Makes her aware of every sound in the vast, dark forest. Assures her that she cannot trust her senses. That even the most innocent sounds—the whirring of the wind in the leaves, a squirrel darting up a tree trunk, a branch breaking in the distance—could be threats in disguise.

And when, after a long time hovering between hallucination and reality, she finally falls asleep, the fever gives shape to these threats and lets her dreams be haunted by bears, snakes, police officers ... and the ghost of her best friend.

Chapter Twenty

As Rose forces her eyes open the next morning, the sun has only just begun to paint orange-red strokes in the clouds of the sky, and it will take several hours before its rays reach her face. Nevertheless, daylight feels like drops of hydrochloric acid in her eyes.

This is her first sensory impression. The next is the sweet, slightly nauseating smell of pine and resin, which fills her nostrils and reminds her where she is.

With it comes a profound sense of powerlessness that almost makes her cry.

Every joint in her body hurts from the fever, especially her neck, and she can almost hear it creak as she glances down at her thigh.

Not surprisingly, the wound has only gotten worse overnight. The splinter is surrounded by swollen, reddish skin, and at the bottom of the scab, thick, glistening bubbles of yellowish pus trickle forth when she presses on the skin around the wound. On one side of the hole in the jeans, the fabric has almost merged with the scab. It's disgusting, but she doesn't dare pull it loose out of fear that it will start bleeding again.

"Sebastian?" she mumbles in a rusty voice she barely recognizes as her own. "Are you awake?"

She turns her fever-heavy head so she can look down at him—and receives another shot of pain in her neck.

"Sebastian?"

"Uh-huh, yeah."

After those words, there is a pause. Then he lets out a noise that is somewhere between a sigh and a gasp, which she assumes must mean he also remembered where they are.

Now he rolls over on his side and lifts his head, enabling her to see his face. His blond hair is messy, he has bluish-gray bags under his eyes, and his skin is pale as wax. He looks awful. As if he's spent months out here instead of just one night.

"You don't look too good."

"Hate to say it, Sis, but you don't exactly look like a top model right now either," he replies dryly as he sits up and looks around. "Man, I'm so thirsty."

Only now that he's put it into words does Rose—

and perhaps her brain too—realize that the same goes for her. She is thirsty.

No, she's more than just thirsty. She is *parched.* Completely drained.

"We should have gathered water yesterday when it rained," Sebastian sighs.

Rose nods and lets her gaze drift up to the sky. There are dark clouds, but they're some distance away, and she's not sure if they're moving in their direction.

"We'll make it back to the river today," she says. "I promise."

She tries to sound convincing and confident. Apparently, though, it doesn't work very well, because Sebastian stares at her with the same skeptical look he has when they're playing Trivial Pursuit at home and she has answered something he doesn't think she should be able to.

What his snide comment would have been, however, she will never know, because just then, the echo of a distant bang ripples through the woods, causing them both to flinch.

A weapon that was fired. Rose is certain, and Sebastian's eyes reveal that he agrees.

It's too far away for it to be them that are being shot at, but that's not much of a consolation, because she has a disquieting hunch about what the sound means.

"Were ... were you the only one who got away from the bus?" she asks gently.

"I don't know how many because I was in a hurry to get down to the water to get to you, but I think I saw a few running into the woods. They were ..."

He hesitates for a moment, then widens his eyes as he comprehends Rose's logic; That the shots could have come from the soldiers who have caught up with —and perhaps executed—one of the escaped children.

"We can't be sure if it's them," she hastens to say, but it's too late. Sebastian simply shakes his head and crawls out of the shelter. Once out, he wipes his eyes with the sleeve of his jacket and gets up.

"I'd like to get out of here."

Rose nods and crawls out to join him, after which she pulls herself up ... on fever-weak legs that almost aren't able to carry her weight anymore.

Chapter Twenty-One

Two hours later, Rose still hasn't been able to keep her promise. The only water they've found is that which is bound in the forest floor, turning the next stretch into a soft and mushy marshland broken only by sporadic mounds and fallen tree trunks.

If they wanted to, they could go around, but neither of them does as it seems to be a pretty long detour. Furthermore, they've heard two more shots since the first. Both seeming to be significantly closer.

"Give me your hand," Sebastian says, stepping onto a moss-covered tree trunk leading to the nearest mound.

Rose takes his hand but not before taking a moment to assess whether it's absolutely necessary. Because although he refuses to admit it, she has noticed that Sebastian has also started to show signs of fever. It's not as evident as it is with her, and it's probably mainly due to his dehydration, but his reflexes seem dulled, and he sometimes struggles to keep his balance.

"Oh, come on, that's just gross," he exclaims, as he steps onto the mound.

"What's gross?"

He responds by pointing down at a strip of grass at the foot of the mound. In the center of it lies a dark brown lump of fur. At first, Rose can't identify it. Then she sees the paws, the scut … and the neck where the head should have been.

"What is it?" Sebastian asks.

"A rabbit, I think," Rose replies, before adding, inside herself: *The more troubling question is what did that to it.*

Some distance behind them, something makes the leaves of a bush move with a crackling sound. Could be that it's just the wind, but nevertheless, the effect of the sound is clear: Rose and Sebastian freeze in place, after which they look at each other nervously and quickly move on.

This was a stupid idea, Rose thinks as they balance their way from mound to mound on fallen logs and half-buried rocks. *We should have gone around.*

As a kind of silent confirmation of that thought, the swampy forest floor grabs her sneaker as she steps down on a pile of damp leaves and pulls downward, covering most of her shoe in mud.

Wet, sticky, and disgusting mud.

Instinctively, she pulls her foot upward, but that only makes it worse, as the sudden movement causes the shoe to slip off her ankle. It stays in the mud while she loses her balance, staggers backward, drops her walking stick, and ends up stomping her shoeless heel in the ground to keep from falling.

"Whoa, what's going on?" Sebastian asks, turning to face her.

"My s-shoe," Rose says between whimpers and moans. "It slipped off."

For a split second, a shadow passes over Sebastian's face, making him look like someone who has lost the last vestige of hope. Then, the resignation in his eyes is replaced by determination.

He walks over, bends down, pulls her sneaker out of the mud, and hands it to her.

"Here."

She wipes her eyes and accepts it, then wipes her foot on a small cluster of grass and presses it into her shoe. It makes a squelching sound as it slides into place, and she can feel the mud creeping up the sock on both sides.

"Thanks," she mumbles.

"Do you need a break before we move on?"

Rose shakes her head, and Sebastian turns toward the next grassy mound on the obstacle course. However, he only manages to take a single step before Rose grabs his arm.

"What?"

Instead of answering with words, Rose points down to where her shoe sank into the muddy forest floor.

The footprint is about three inches deep—and the bottom half of the hole is full of water.

It's brownish, and the surface is filled with small, dark grains that look like coffee grounds. Nevertheless, the sight of the water makes Rose's stomach clench in longing.

"Can ... can we drink it?" Sebastian asks, squinting his eyes as if hoping to determine the quality of the water simply by staring at it. His voice—shaky and hoarse—reveals that he, like her, must make an effort not to throw himself onto the ground and drink directly from the hole.

"Hand me my cane, will you?" Rose says, holding out her hand.

Sebastian bends down, picks up the stick, and hands it to her.

With renewed strength, born of the hope of relieving their thirst, Rose lifts the cane with her feverish hands and hammers one end into the ground a bit left of the footprint. Afterward, she twists it from side to side, forming a triangular hole before pulling it back up.

During the first hopeful seconds, nothing happens. Then small droplets of water start to trickle out from the sides of the hole. Rose looks around and spots a crescent-shaped leaf. She picks it up and gently bends its edges. Next, she kneels in front of the hole and fills the improvised spoon with water.

Calling it clean would be an outright lie, but at least this water is less murky than the water in the footprint, and it's not filled with grains of dirt. Besides, Rose is so thirsty that even this dubious spring seems like a present from a higher power.

Cautiously, she takes a sip. It tastes like dirt and has a nauseatingly pungent aftertaste. None of that matters, though, when held up against the wave of relief spreading throughout her dehydrated body.

"Give it a try," she says, handing the wet leaf spoon to her little brother. "It's not that bad."

Sebastian looks skeptical but doesn't hesitate for long before kneeling down to take a sip as well.

"Not that bad?" he groans, frowning. Still, despite this protest, he immediately takes another sip after the first. Then one more.

It's not a miracle cure against the fever or the infection in Rose's wounds, or the complete exhaustion of their bodies, for that matter, but the water gives them a bright spot to cling to. A modest flame of joy and hope in a world that seems to sink deeper and deeper into a gray darkness.

This flame of hope is allowed to burn for about twenty minutes. Then the soothing effect of the water in their stomachs is replaced by a searing pain that brings them to their knees on the damp forest floor and forces them to vomit.

Chapter Twenty-Two

Afternoon, soon evening again, and nothing has changed for the better. Hunger growls in their stomachs like a predator lurking in the shadows. Their feverish hands grope in empty pockets again and again, without learning the lesson.

There *is* no food and no water. Only dizziness, nausea, and an increasing paranoia that has them glancing back over their shoulder every time the wind shakes the treetops and causes the dark kaleidoscope of shadows on the ground below them to turn.

And the mosquitoes. They're also back at work, running their little shifts, commuting back and forth between this walking self-service buffet and wherever those little bloodsucking beasts stay when they're off duty.

"It's hopeless," Sebastian sighs behind Rose's back. "We're never getting out of here."

His voice sounds hoarse, raspy, and she's not sure if he's talking to her or to himself. To be fair, though, she's also not sure if she's actually articulating her answer—that they have to keep putting one foot in front of the other—or if she's only saying it inside her own head.

That's how confused she is. The line between reality and fever dream almost doesn't exist anymore, neither for her nor for Sebastian. The only thing she knows for certain at this point is that they're not alone out here in the increasing darkness of the forest.

Someone—or something—is on their heels. Keeping an eye on them. And she's no longer sure it's just the soldiers they have to worry about because several times she has heard something moving rapidly across the forest floor behind them. Faster than any two-legged creature would be capable of.

There are wolves in these woods, a voice whispers in the back of her mind. *You know that, right?*

Yeah, but there are also deer, foxes, rabbits, and all kinds of other harmless, four-legged animals, she protests inside herself. It doesn't help much, though, because now that the seed has been planted in her mind, her brain insists that the jarring howls reverberating through the forest don't just come from the wind.

She tries to speed up but immediately regrets it when a hot powder keg detonates in the wound on her thigh, setting her entire nervous system ablaze.

She looks down and is overwhelmed by a powerlessness she can hardly bear. The skin surrounding the splinter is no longer ruddy from budding inflammation. It's bluish-purple, swollen, and carries a nasty marbling of dried-out, yellowish pus. If it's not cleaned and treated soon, it'll—

No further does she get before a sound from a bush to her right freezes her thoughts as well as her body.

A deep, guttural growl. The sound is unmistakable, and even before her gaze has found its way over there, she knows, without a flicker of doubt, what it will find.

Correct. They are right there. Two eyes, hovering in the darkness between the tree trunks, glistening faintly in the glow of the cloudy firmament above them.

"Sebastian," she whispers.

"I see it," he replies.

Rose's fingers clutch her walking stick as she slowly steps to the side, moving closer to her little brother. Not that it will make any difference. If the wolf decides to attack, her improvised weapon will be nothing more than a mild annoyance to it. Because neither her nor Sebastian have the strength to use the stick as a club. Besides, there are probably more yellow eyes hiding out there in the dark.

Now the beast growls again. A deep, menacing sound that awakens something—a primordial instinct of some kind, perhaps—in the far reaches of Rose's mind and makes her quiver uncontrollably. In part out of fear, in part out of shame because she has failed her duty and can't protect her little brother.

"Go away," she orders, but the words come out as nothing more than a half-choked whisper. "Get lost, you stupid beast!"

She moves her arm up and down in a sweeping motion, hoping it will scare the beast, but it doesn't work. If anything, it has the opposite effect, as the wolf growls louder and its eyes grow larger. It's moving toward them. Slowly, yes, but it *is* getting closer. Soon it will step out into the light so they can see its face. And its teeth.

Rose's pulse is pounding so hard in her temples that it feels like her head is about to explode, and she has a hard time catching—and holding on to—a single useful thought.

Then she sees it. On the ground next to her foot; a loose stone the size of a golf ball.

Carefully—so very carefully—she drops to one knee, leaning on the cane with one hand and reaching for the stone with the other.

At the exact moment her fingers close around the stone, a terrifying, pearly-white set of teeth appears beneath the hovering eyes. Around them, the rest of the animal's head manifests: Lips, vibrating in time with its growl. A muzzle whose nostrils alternately expand and contract. Ears lying down, almost completely flat against its disheveled, black fur.

Aware that she has to act if she isn't to be completely paralyzed by fear, Rose clutches the stone and discreetly lifts it up along her hip. Next, she pulls her arm backward and takes aim.

Behind her, she hears Sebastian take a deep breath and hold it in. She does the same—except she only holds the air in for a brief second before letting it out again, accompanied by a desperate scream of exertion.

All her remaining strength is put into the throw, and yet the result is pathetic. The stone hits the animal's shoulder with a dull thud and then falls to the ground, not having achieved anything at all. The monster hasn't budged an inch.

Rose, on the other hand, starts to sway unsteadily back and forth as if she had just been hit by something heavy. She tries to prevent it by leaning on the stick, but the forest floor keeps tilting from side to side like a ship's deck in stormy weather, and the fall is inevitable. Her back hits the dry leaves and twigs of the forest floor with a crunching sound.

She opens her mouth and looks at her little brother, wanting to tell him to run away, but she is unable to let out anything but a horrified gasp as her gaze slips past him.

There is a figure standing in the shadows behind Sebastian. A large man with what looks like a long metal rod resting on one shoulder. Except it's not a rod. It's the barrel of a rifle.

No, not like this! It can't end like this!

But it will. She is going to end her days here, and the very last thing she will get to see in this world will be Sebastian's execution. The soldier is going to blow his brain out right in front of her, and she will lie here, unable to do anything but stare at her little brother's corpse while she herself is being chewed to pieces by the wolf. This is how it's going to end, and there's nothing she—

"What is it, Rocky? What did you find?" says the figure behind Sebastian, and although Rose is already so far down the path to unconsciousness that she is no longer able to decode the meaning of the words, she is awake enough to be confused at the gentle, almost friendly sound of the voice.

And this confusion is the last thing that fills her foggy mind before the world fades out and she sinks into darkness.

PART THREE

The Cabin

"It's not my own death I fear the most."

O. E. Geralt

Chapter Twenty-Three

It's the faint rasping sound that pulls her out of her sleep. It comes from the curtains that scrape against the wall every time the wind reaches its invisible hand through the half-open window and pushes them.

She's no longer in the woods. She is lying on an old, worn leather sofa, wrapped in a thick blanket that smells of dust and old tobacco smoke.

She blinks a few times to get her tired eyes to focus properly, then lets her gaze drift around the rest of the room. The first thing it finds is an old ceiling lamp, the yellow-brown shade of which is decorated with thin threads of cobwebs. From there, her gaze moves to a wall adorned with taxidermy mounts. Stuffed animals staring stiffly at her with their creepy, lifeless glass eyes. Below them is a stove whose glass doors are sooty and flicker with a warm, orange glow from the flames inside.

Only now, as it lifts its head and looks at her, does she notice the dog on the floor. It's a large black Labrador lying on a folded carpet slightly to the left of the stove.

And it is, those squinted eyes tell her, the same dog that nearly scared her to death last night because her fever-addled brain had transformed it into a murderous wolf.

As it lies there now, two large paws resting on the floor in front of it, head slightly tilted, it no longer scares her. In fact, it looks kind.

The place, on the other hand—this strange wooden cabin that she has no idea how she ended up in—still makes her uneasy. Especially since she can't see Sebastian anywhere.

A sudden impulse hits her. She grabs the blanket and lifts it up so she can see her leg.

Her suspicion was correct. The wood splinter has been removed from her thigh. Where it was now sits a wide, white bandage.

Gently she touches the dressing. It's flawless, not too tight and not too loose. Whoever put it on knew what he or she was doing.

"It's best to not touch it," says a male voice behind

her. "I've cleaned and stitched it as best I could, but I'm not a professional."

Rose turns her face and looks in the direction of the sound. It's the man who turned up last night. Then, he stood in the shadows behind Sebastian with a rifle resting on his shoulder. Now he is standing in the doorway into what must be the cabin's kitchen, with a plate and a glass of water in his hands. A large man with a short-trimmed, light gray beard and friendly eyes in the same brown color as the flannel shirt he is wearing.

"My little brother?"

"The guesthouse," the man replies, nodding toward the half-open window. "There wasn't really room for both of you in here. But don't worry, he's fine. He's sleeping."

"So ... you're not one of the soldiers?"

"I'm not sure I understand what you're asking," the man says, tilting his head in exactly the same way the dog did when it studied her earlier. "I mean, if you're asking because of the rifle, I'm a hunter."

"Never mind," Rose says, shaking her head. "I'd like to see my brother."

She tries to sit up on the sofa but is immediately flooded by a wave of dizziness.

"I'd suggest that you get your energy up a little first," the man says as he walks over and places the glass of water and the plate on the coffee table in front of her. There is food on the plate, a ham sandwich. "And as I said, your brother is okay. He went out like a light as soon as he lay down, even though he insisted he wouldn't close an eye all night."

He hesitates a little, rubs his cheek, and then adds:

"He also needs to recuperate a bit, don't you think?"

Rose looks at the man, at the dog, then around the cabin, and finally down at the bandage on her thigh. All four things suggest that this strange man doesn't mean them any harm. In fact, he probably saved her life by bringing her here.

"Listen," he says. "I get that you're a bit on your toes. I would be too, in your shoes. But how about we meet halfway and say that you take a moment to eat your food? And when you're done, I'll wake up your brother and bring him over here. How does that sound?"

A moment of contemplation. Then Rose nods.

"Good," the man says, smiling. "I'm John, by the way, and the big furry guy on the floor there is Rocky. He was the one who found you. Isn't that right, Rocky? It was you who got the wind of ...?"

At the sound of his name, Rocky lifts his head and stares at his owner with big, gullible Scooby Doo eyes, his tail whipping from side to side on the floor behind him. That she could mistake this dog for a ferocious wolf strikes her as downright silly this morning.

Realizing that the hunter is still waiting for her to say her name, she raises a hand apologetically.

"Rose, um ... my name is Rose. And my brother is Sebastian."

"It's nice to meet you, Rose," John says, gesturing down to the plate. "And let's try to get something in that stomach, shall we?"

Rose purses her lips in a frozen smile and nods, then reaches for the food.

"I will. Thank you ... for my thigh too."

"Don't mention it," he replies, making a sweeping motion with his hand. "I had to do something."

With that, the hunter turns his back on her and walks back into the kitchen. In the meantime, Rose starts to eat her sandwich. It hurts in her stomach when she swallows the first bite ... but it also wakes it up, overwhelming her with an almost unbearable hunger and thirst—and in next to no time, both the sandwich and the water are gone.

"What were you kids doing all alone that far out in the woods anyway?" he asks from the kitchen. "Did you get lost or something?"

"Yeah, that too," Rose replies, staring blankly down at her hands as all the highlights of yesterday's trip through hell flicker by inside her head. "We were on the run."

"On the run? From who?"

His voice isn't exactly distrustful, but it's certainly spiced with skepticism ... which makes Rose realize something: The man in the kitchen has no idea what's been going on out in the world.

"You don't know, do you?" she asks.

Now John's face reappears in the doorway. A face whose puzzled expression is enough to answer the question.

"Know what?"

"That it's chaos out there. It's all broken down. All of it. People are getting killed for no reason, and ... and nobody cares. My best friend, Kitty, she ..."

Rose doesn't get any further before the words fade and are reduced to incomprehensible sobbing sounds.

In an attempt to gain control of herself, she presses her hands against her temples and closes her eyes. When she opens them again, John is no longer standing in the doorway into the kitchen. He has walked over to the stove, from where he is staring at her with an expression she can't read.

For a long time, he remains there, silent as the grave, with his thumbs resting behind the waistband of his jeans. Then he goes over to the coffee table, picks up the glass and the empty plate, and carries them into the kitchen, saying:

"So, what exactly are we talking about? Terrorist attacks? Civil war? Frankly, neither would come as a big surprise."

Rose opens her mouth to tell him that she doesn't think it's one or the other. However, she doesn't have time to say anything before John speaks again. And when that happens, his words leave her speechless and drenched in panic.

"I guess that would also explain why I couldn't get through to the emergency center until this morning," are the words he says.

Chapter Twenty-Four

The timing is chilling. At the exact moment that the potential consequences of John's decision to call 911 start to explode like fireworks in Rose's head, the sound of a car engine emerges outside the cabin.

Groaning with exertion, she pushes herself up from the couch, staggers over to the window—whose curtains are now bathed alternately in blue and red light —and gets her horrible premonition confirmed.

In the hunting cabin's small, graveled driveway— which is little more than a slight extension of the winding dirt road leading into it—two vehicles are parked. One, a dark blue SUV, must be John's.

The second is a patrol car.

"What's up?" John asks behind her, but she doesn't

bother to answer him. She just continues to stare in increasing terror at the police car.

At the man behind the wheel, who is now getting out.

"Oh, please God, no. Not him!"

His bloodstained uniform is more worn and wrinkled than it was when she last saw him. So is his face, in a way. Still, she easily recognizes him.

Officer Mendez. Sheriff Hodge's young assistant who locked her and Kitty in the gym—and who brutally executed Mrs. Shanahan by imprisoning her in the back of a burning patrol car.

"The rifle," she hisses, after which she turns around and looks at John. "Your rifle! Where is it?"

"Whoa, whoa, whoa," he says, holding his hands up in front of him. "Let's keep our heads on straight. After all, I called for them myself."

"YOUR RIFLE!" Rose roars. "I NEED IT!"

John takes a step back and stares at her in amazement. Behind him, Rocky is also on his feet. He looks just as confused as his owner.

"Listen, I can see you're scared," John says, annoyingly calmly. "And that's no wonder, with everything you and your brother have been through. But you also have to try to see it from my point of view, okay? You're asking me to go get my rifle because there is an ambulance in the driveway ... an ambulance which, by the way, I called for."

"It's *not* an ambulance," Rose says, pointing to the window. "It's a patrol car. And the officer out there is a psychopath. He tried to kill me and my friend. And he killed one of my teachers and made us watch. Christ, her blood is still on his uniform!"

A pause. Then John takes a few steps backward so he can look out the window. Once he has done so, he nods slowly, after which he turns around and walks out into the kitchen. Whether that means he's buying her story or not, Rose isn't sure, but she doesn't really care either. As long as he finds a weapon for them, she is happy.

He does. He appears in the doorway again, this time with his rifle in his hands, at the exact same second that the first knocks sound from the front door.

"Hello? Anybody home?"

The sound of Mendez' voice, even with such harmless words, makes it all come back to Rose, and she has to bite her lip not to break down in tears.

"Hello?" he repeats. "It's the police! We've received an emergency call from this address. Is anyone here?"

John gives her a *you stay put* look, and when she has nodded her yes, he raises his voice and shouts:

"Just a sec! I'm on my way!"

After those words, he nods to Rose one final time

before leaving the room, with Rocky on his heels. Meanwhile, Rose crawls into hiding behind the couch —and concentrates on listening.

"Good morning," she hears John say in the hallway. "Sorry about the wait. You caught me on the can. Typical, right?"

"Sure," the officer replies in a tone of voice that says he finds this information neither interesting nor entertaining. "And that thing?"

"Oh, don't mind that. It's habit when I hear a car in the driveway out here in the middle of nowhere. It's nothing personal. I don't even think it's loaded."

"I see. As long as you don't point it at me. You called 911?"

A long pause. Then John clears his throat.

"Um, yeah. Yes, I did, but ... turns out it was all a big misunderstanding." He lets out a nervous chuckle. "I heard someone screaming in the woods behind the house, and it sounded pretty bad. So, I decided it was probably better to be on the safe side and call for help."

Another pause. An awkward one. Rose can easily sense this, even though she isn't part of the conversation.

"I'll admit I do feel a little silly," John continues.

"It was an animal?" the officer says.

"A deer. It got caught in the fence behind the cabin. But I'm telling you, it sounded just like a person."

"I understand," Mendez says. "But I hope you also understand that I have to check the place out anyway. Emergency calls must be taken seriously. Can I come in?"

"Uh, yeah. Of course, but ... it happened out in the backyard, and the deer isn't even there anymore. It got free."

"No need to get jumpy. I just have to do a quick sweep and make sure everything is okay. It's protocol, nothing more."

Those words are followed by another pause, during which no words are exchanged between the two men. In return, the sound of creaking floorboards tells Rose that they are on their way into the living room. From her seat behind the couch, she can't see them, but she can see Rocky, who has returned to the room and is sitting next to the stove. And by following the dog's gaze, she can roughly make out where the two men are in relation to her.

"It's a nice place you've got here," Mendez says in a voice completely devoid of actual interest.

"It's nice, yeah, but the cabin isn't mine, though. I rent it every now and then for a week or two. To get away from it all, you know. It's a great place to go hunting."

"I can imagine. How many bedrooms does it have?"

"One here in the cabin and one in the guesthouse out there."

"And yet you choose to sleep here, in the living room?"

Behind the couch, Rose grimaces. Mendez isn't dumb. His question was a trap because he had spotted the blanket and the pillow on the couch—and John walked right into it.

"And out there we have the kitchen, I guess?"

Without giving John a chance to answer, Mendez marches through the living room and into the kitchen —and Rose barely manages to pull her legs in so he doesn't spot her in passing.

"There are *two* dirty plates in the sink ...?"

He's messing with him, Rose thinks, feeling the hairs on her neck rise. *And he sounds like he's enjoying himself.*

"One of them belongs to Rocky," John replies promptly. "That's my dog. He usually gets my leftovers on a plate."

No answer. Only the sound of a door creaking.

"Bedroom?"

"Yup," John confirms. "Listen, I don't mean to be rude, but ... is there something in particular you're looking for? I have some appointments today that I'd rather not be late for."

Mendez lets out a mix between a snort and a chuckle.

"Don't worry," he says. "I'm done in here now. As I said, it's just something we have to do. A routine check to make sure everything is in order. That said, I'd also like to take a quick look at your guesthouse out there. Would you mind tagging along and unlocking it for me?"

"Well, sure, but ... it's not locked."

"No? Well, I guess I don't really need you anymore, then," Mendez says coldly, and then—before Rose even has time to understand the meaning of his words—a faint click sounds, followed by two deafening bangs.

Instinctively, she curls up and closes her eyes. When she opens them again, it's to the sight of John's face hitting the floor just to the left of the couch. His eyes wide open and devoid of life, his mouth filled with a foamy mixture of blood and spit.

On the other side of her hiding place, a series of new sounds erupt. A ferocious alternation between high-pitched barks and a deep, bestial snarling.

"OUCH, DAMMIT! LET GO OF ME, YOU FUCKING MUTT!"

Get him, Rocky! Rose screams inside herself with such intensity and determination that you'd think she actually believed herself able to communicate with the dog via telepathy. *Tear that psycho apart!*

The dog tries its best. Of that, the sounds leave no

doubt, but even the sharpest of teeth and the strongest jaw don't stand a chance against a loaded gun.

Thus, Rocky ends his days wheezing and whimpering on the living room floor next to his owner, while Officer Mendez leaves the cabin and walks toward the guesthouse.

Toward Sebastian.

Chapter Twenty-Five

There is no time to think. There's only time to act—
and that's what Rose does. She crawls out of her hiding
place, past the hunter and his loyal dog, both of whom
have let out their last, gurgling moans now. Two more
lives lost, because of her.

But these will be the last. This she promises herself
as she grabs the rifle from the floor and gets on her
feet. She's still weak and lightheaded, and the wound in
her thigh is throbbing badly, but her body is pumped
full of adrenaline, and she plans to use that to the
fullest.

She raises the rifle and presses its buttstock against
her shoulder, just like her dad taught her and Sebastian when they were younger and shot at empty soda
cans in the backyard with a pellet gun. This rifle is

heavier, a lot heavier, but the principle remains the same, and she feels she has a reasonable aim. Especially given that her current target is far bigger than an empty Coke can.

Knowing that she can't afford to waste time, she runs out into the hallway of the cabin and then to the front door. It's ajar. She pushes it open with her shoulder and hurries down the two steps in front of the door while turning the barrel of the rifle toward the center of the driveway and taking aim.

Mendez is gone. He has vanished in the gray morning mist ... and the door to the guesthouse is still closed. Could he really have made it all the way in there so—

A sharp pain flares up in the back of her head, causing black spots to appear in her field of vision as he grabs her hair and pulls her backward.

"I had a feeling I'd get to see you again," he hisses into her ear, after which he pushes her up against the outer wall and hammers a fist into her stomach. "Where's your friend? The, um ... cat girl. Kitty? Was that it?"

"She's d-dead," Rose groans.

Mendez grabs her arm and pulls it violently from side to side until she loses her grip on the rifle, causing it to fall to the ground. Next, he moves his other hand from her hair down to her neck.

"Just how stupid do you think I am?" he asks. "The emergency call said there were two wounded out here. Not one, but two! So where is she?"

"She ... is dead!" Rose repeats. "It's just me left."

Mendez tightens his grip on her neck and stares at her with his dark brown eyes. *Studies* her.

"A truth and a lie," he then says. "Your friend may be gone ... but you're *not* alone out here. You're protecting someone."

The shock of being read so easily hits Rose like a bucket of ice-cold water, and before she knows it, her eyes have betrayed her by wandering toward the guesthouse. Mendez sees it and pulls his chapped lips up in a smile.

"I'll make you watch," he whispers, tightening his grasp even harder around her neck. So hard that she's on the verge of passing out. "I'll break your legs so you can't run, and then you'll get to watch as I put a bullet in the forehead of your secret buddy."

With those words, he yanks her sideways and lets go, causing her to stumble across the driveway before falling helplessly to the ground.

Now she's lying there, gasping for breath, staring up at the gray sky, listening to the sound of the officer's steps resounding in the gravel beneath her as he comes closer.

Get up! she orders herself. *Sebastian needs you!*

Trembling with pain, she rolls to her stomach and tries to push herself up. However, she barely manages to put her hands in the gravel before a new sound drowns out Mendez' footsteps—and it hits her like an adrenaline shot in the heart.

"LEAVE HER ALONE!" Sebastian roars in a voice that is an eerie blend of shock and horror. "LEAVE HER ALONE OR I'LL SHOOT!"

Rose looks up and sees her little brother standing by the cabin's front door. He is pale, and his hands shake so much that the barrel of the rifle is dancing up and down in random patterns in the air in front of him.

"Think it through, kid," Mendez says, his calm voice an uncanny contrast to Sebastian's. "Loading a rifle like that takes time. Even if you had more bullets, you'd only have time for one shot. *One*. You're seriously planning to—"

That's as far as he gets before the bang comes.

Chapter Twenty-Six

It could have ended there. The bullet from John's hunting rifle could have penetrated Officer Mendez' heart, allowing the fragile hope of a somewhat happy ending for Rose and her little brother to live on for a little longer.

But.

The bullet does not strike the officer's ice-cold heart, and it penetrates nothing. It strafes his upper arm, leaving a small rip in the sleeve of his uniform. That's all.

Now he stands there, his eyes fixed on Sebastian, who pointlessly keeps pulling at the rifle's charging handle—perhaps in the irrational hope of finding an extra bullet in there. The psychopath says nothing; he just stares quietly as reality slowly dawns on the boy.

He hasn't even drawn his service pistol—and Rose has a terrible suspicion as to why that is.

No, it's more than a suspicion. She *knows* why. It won't be satisfactory. It will take more than a quick death to give the deviants a suitable punishment for all the trouble they've caused. It will take *pain*, and it will take *remorse*.

As if he's heard this thought in Rose's head, Mendez turns around, takes three quick steps toward her, and gives her a kick in the stomach. He then shifts his attention back to her little brother while she's lying on the gravel coughing up blood.

Through a flickering, gray veil of fog, she sees Sebastian drop the rifle and flee into the cabin, closely pursued by Mendez.

He doesn't stand a chance, she thinks. *We don't stand a chance.*

Ensuing that thought, a series of events flickers before her inner eye in short flashes. She sees Mendez dragging their lifeless bodies out to the patrol car and stuffing them in the trunk. She sees him driving into town, whistling cheerfully and drumming his fingers on the steering wheel. She sees him stop in front of their mom's house, and—oh God—she sees him hanging their bodies in a lamppost on the street, just like the dead man they saw earlier. A macabre work of art. A monument to serve as an eternal reminder of how she failed Sebastian.

This last image hits her hard. Harder than the kick in her stomach, and harder than the burning sensation in her lungs. And it's in this image she finds the strength to once again place her shivering hands in the gravel and push herself up.

Fueled by anger, she fights her way up to her knees and from there all the way to her feet. Her stomach hurts—hell, *everything* hurts—but she swallows the pain and staggers across the driveway toward the open door into the cabin.

She can hear them in there. It sounds like one of them is banging fiercely on a door. Perhaps that's a good sign. It could mean that Sebastian has bought some time by locking himself in the bathroom.

For a hopeful second, that's what Rose thinks before she enters the room and gets the right explanation.

The loud banging doesn't come from any of the doors. It comes from the wooden floor every time the involuntary convulsions of Sebastian's body cause the heels of his shoes to hammer down on the planks.

His eyes are white, his face bluish and swollen. He lies on his back, squirming uncontrollably beneath the weight of Mendez, who has both hands closed around his neck.

Desperate to come to her brother's rescue, Rose lets her gaze drift around the living room until it stops on the fire poker hanging on a rack next to the stove. She stumbles over there, grabs it, then continues toward Mendez while lifting the weapon above her head.

He's got his back turned, and he's so immersed in squeezing the life out of the deviant that he doesn't even notice her presence.

That suits her just fine. Because she's not planning on giving him any warning this time, and she's not going to show mercy.

The first blow buries the fire poker's hook in the left side of his neck and opens the main artery, creating a fountain of blood that soaks his shoulder. The subsequent blow sinks the hook into his temple, causing him to topple sideways and fall to the floor. At some level, Rose realizes that this is the pivotal blow —the one that ensures Mendez will never get up again—yet she keeps pounding away with the fire poker. Over and over, she strikes until she can barely lift her weapon anymore—and only then does she sink to her knees on the wooden floor next to her little brother.

"Sebastian?" she says, shaking him.

No answer.

"Sebastian! Wake up! It's over. He can't hurt you anymore."

She shakes him again, harder, but still gets no answer.

"Wake up!" she repeats in a voice that gradually loses strength. "Come on, Sebastian. We have to go home. We have to ..."

Nothing. His eyes are blank, expressionless, and the soft crackle of the stove is the only sound to be heard in the cabin. Like a symbolic backdrop—the last embers burning out—it lies in the background as the crushing realization dawns in Rose's mind.

Chapter Twenty-Seven

It's raining again. Large, heavy drops relentlessly whipping down, leaving small, crater-like depressions on the surface of the two fresh piles of dirt in the garden behind the cabin.

She meant to make three graves instead of just the two, but she had to acknowledge that she simply didn't have the strength to do so. Therefore, John shares his final resting place with Rocky while Sebastian has his very own spot under the large oak.

That's also where Rose has spent most of her time in the last twenty-four hours. First digging his grave, then staring at it. If she didn't have anything else to do, she could probably sit there forever, just waiting to die of starvation.

But Rose still has one thing left on her to-do list.

On that account, she now takes one last look at the grave and at Sebastian's name, which she has carved into the bark of the old oak, after which she gets up and enters the cabin.

On the coffee table in the living room is a brown backpack. She found it in a closet inside John's bedroom. She doesn't think he would mind her borrowing it—nor that she used the last loaf of bread from the kitchen to make the packed lunch at the bottom of the bag.

The lunch isn't the only thing she's packed. There's also a flashlight, a water bottle, a first aid kit—and last, but not least, there's a gun.

It's Mendez' service weapon, which she, with shaking hands, removed from the hip holster of his corpse this morning.

She winces at the memory of that moment. How her imagination insisted that he would open his eyes and grab her hand just as she was about to pull out the gun.

Of course, that didn't happen—and from now on, he definitely won't be grabbing anybody any longer. That would require nothing short of a miracle given that she dumped his lifeless body into the well behind the guesthouse.

After zipping the backpack and hurling it onto her shoulder, Rose continues through the cabin and heads out into the driveway. Both vehicles are still out there, and even now, knowing that Mendez can't harm her anymore, she feels a sting of panic at the sight of the patrol car.

Then again, that might be a healthy instinct to have, she decides. Because even though her brain still can't fully comprehend the change in the world that she's witnessed over the past week, one thing is clear to her: It's no longer a good idea to blindly trust members of the police force.

She found the key to John's old Ford Bronco hanging on a hook in the kitchen, and to her relief, the engine starts on the first try.

Before she puts it into gear and starts driving, she casts one last, melancholy glance at the cabin. Part of her wants to stay here. To hide out here in the woods and let the rest of the world fend for itself.

But that is of no use. She has to go back home, at least for a while, because she has some bad news to deliver, and she wouldn't be able to look herself in the eye if she didn't do that.

PART FOUR

Home

～ઈ

"If the door is never answered,
at some point you will stop knocking."

O. E. GERALT

Chapter Twenty-Eight

They are there, on sidewalks, behind garden fences and windows, but they don't feel like real people. They feel like random extras, filling the backdrop to a movie set.

However, what flashes by on the other side of the rain-soaked windscreen isn't the set of a film. It's the streets of Coulton. The streets of her hometown.

A ghost town. That's what it has become. A rainy ghost town filled with the ghosts of the people who were once Rose's neighbors. Filled with empty canisters.

There are also dead people here. Not as many as she saw when she drove through Pineview on the way here, but enough to make her a bit paranoid. The worst was the sight of Gerald Boyle. He was the local pharmacist, and he was a really kind man. Now he's a corpse in a white coat hanging from the *WELCOME TO COUL-TON* sign at the edge of town.

The local police force has been busy—and Rose has finally figured out why they are doing it. At least she thinks she has. Actually, it's a deeply disturbing thought. She believes they're hanging the dead outside, displaying them like macabre scarecrows—not to scare away other deviants, but to draw them into the light. Because the first impulse of a normal person who spots a dead person hanging from a lamppost will inevitably be to call the police. The problem is that the police are ... well, the problem.

As she turns onto her own street, she feels a growing unease in her stomach. Part of it is because she'll be home soon, and she's nervous about what she'll find there. Another part is the street itself. Because at first glance, everything looks so normal in the small neighborhood. There are lights in the windows and laundry on a clothesline in one of the backyards. A little further ahead she can even see old Harold McGee down from number 27 taking one of his three daily walks with Frankie.

So damned normal. Except, of course, that Harold strolls casually in the pouring rain without an umbrella, resulting in both him and the grumpy old bulldog being drenched. And apparently, not a single person in the entire neighborhood cares about the laundry getting soaked on the clothesline.

When she is three houses away from her own, Rose parks John's SUV at the curb. That way, her house won't be the first to get investigated if an officer comes by and spots the strange vehicle.

After gathering courage for a moment, Rose opens the car door, steps out onto the drenched street, and starts walking toward her childhood home. She doesn't take many steps, though, before she picks up something out of the corner of her eye that makes her stop and gasp.

It's Mrs. Thompson, who always sits on her white porch with her morning coffee, waving at Rose and Sebastian when they pass her house on their way to the bus stop every morning. She is sitting there now as well, in her flowered nightgown and with her morning coffee cup sitting on the table in front of her.

The problem is that it's not morning anymore. It's late afternoon.

How long has she been sitting out here? Rose thinks as she raises her hand and waves hesitantly.

Her greeting isn't returned. Mrs. Thompson does look in her direction, but she doesn't seem to register her at all. In fact, she doesn't seem to register much.

Rose flips the collar of her jacket up around her neck, partly to shield herself from the rain and partly to suppress the chill running over her neck. Truth be told, she doesn't know Mrs. Thompson very well, but that doesn't change the fact that there's something really terrifying about seeing her like this.

As Rose approaches her home, every step feels heavier—and when she stops in front of the driveway, she once again has to take a deep breath to gather the courage to continue.

The garage door is open, and she can see the rear of her mom's blue Kia in there. It hasn't been out—at least not today—because it's completely dry, and there aren't any puddles on the floor either, which there usually are if it's been driven around in the rain.

Actually, there is also a door into the house from the garage, but the light switch is located on the wall all the way in the back, and Rose doesn't feel like moving through the semi-darkness to get there. Therefore, she walks over to the front door instead. It doesn't help much, though, as it's left ajar and gives her exactly the same ominous vibe.

Gently, she pushes the door with her foot. It slowly swings open, inviting her into the hallway.

Throughout Rose's life, this house has been her home. Yet now, standing in this narrow hallway, shrouded in gray darkness, listening to the insistent drumming of rain on the roof, she doesn't feel at home. She feels exposed.

"Mom?" she whispers, and then a little louder, "Are you home?"

No answer.

She continues to the end of the hallway and steps through the open door that leads into the kitchen. Unlike the entrance hall, the kitchen has two large windows, but the curtains are drawn, thus blocking out the daylight they would otherwise have let in. As a result, everything inside the room carries a gloomy ashen hue.

"Mom?" she repeats. "It's me. Are you in here?"

Silence.

Reluctantly, but also with a stubborn intention to do what she came for, while she is still able to muster the courage, she leaves the kitchen and enters the living room.

It's the only illuminated room in the house, and although the light source is modest—the two elongated windows above the couch that let in the dull, gray daylight of the afternoon—Rose has to squint her eyes to adjust to the brightness.

The living room is also empty, and for a moment she considers the possibility that the same might apply to the rest of the house. She felt so sure seeing her mom's car in the garage, but of course, it being out there doesn't necessarily mean that—

Her stream of thought is broken as her gaze wanders through the rain-soaked glass of the window.

Her mom is in the garden. She's sitting on her knees by the flowerbed in front of the terrace. She's wearing her apron and garden hat, and she's holding garden shears in her hand ... but she doesn't use them. She just sits with them while she stares blankly down at the flowers.

She is drenched. Her clothes cling to her crouched body, and jets of water pour from the brim of her hat.

With the sound of her own pulse pounding in her ear canals, Rose sprints out into the utility room at the back of the house, rips open the door to the garden, and continues out onto the wet grass. It's slippery and she's dangerously close to falling, but she doesn't care.

"M-Mom!" she stammers. "Mom, what are you doing?"

Her mom doesn't respond. She is still sitting there, hunched in front of the flowers as if she were just one of the figurines that are spread around the garden.

Once Rose has reached her, she grabs her shoulders and shakes them—at first softly, then a little harder—hoping it will break the trance. It doesn't.

"Mom, it's me," she sobs in a voice so faint that the words almost disappear behind the sound of the raindrops up on the roof. "What's wrong with you?"

While she speaks, Rose carefully grabs the garden

shears and wrestles them free of her mom's fingers. That doesn't trigger any reaction either.

"You're completely soaked, Mom. Come on, we need to get you inside where it's warm."

Gently, she grabs her mom's wrist and lifts her arm up on her own shoulders. Next, she grabs her waist and pulls her up. To her relief, she comes along without resisting—both when she helps her up and when she leads her in the direction of the house.

Half an hour later, they are both sitting on the couch in the living room. Her mom, still silent as a churchyard, is wrapped in a blanket and a comforter that Rose found in her bedroom.

Normally, Rose wouldn't be bothered in the slightest by them sitting next to each other in silence like this, but at this moment, the silence feels like torture.

"Would you like a hot cup of coffee?" she asks, trying to break it.

For a split second, her mom seems to react to the sound of her voice, turning her face slightly, but it may have been a coincidence … and given that nothing more happens, that's probably the explanation.

"Mom, I …" she begins, but before she gets any further in the sentence, a mocking voice—sounding suspiciously like Kitty's—appears in the back of her mind.

Your mom is not here anymore, it says. *Whatever that is, it's not your mom.*

Rose folds her hands and holds them up in front of her mouth for a moment, focusing on keeping both her emotions in check and her late best friend out of her head.

"I have to tell you something," she continues. "It's about Sebastian. He's ... he's dead, Mom."

Her throat constricts, forcing her to pause involuntarily—and as she does, her gaze returns to her mom's green eyes.

No tears, no shock, no grief ... not even confusion.

"Do you hear what I'm saying, Mom? He is *dead*. Sebastian is dead. He was k-killed."

Nothing. She might as well be talking to the armchair on the other side of the coffee table.

With that realization comes the deepest feeling of loneliness Rose has ever had. She is sitting here, next to the person who, of all people in the world, should understand her grief best—and who should be her greatest comfort.

And still, she is all alone.

Chapter Twenty-Nine

She can't stay here. Deep down, she's been aware of it ever since the day she came back home and found her mom out in the garden. That's almost three weeks ago now. Three weeks in which Rose has done her best to take care of her. She feeds her, she washes her, she dresses her, and she talks to her as if she were still her mom.

She is not, though. She might still look like Betty Lavine, some version of her, at least, but even in the few bright moments when she lifts her head and actually looks at Rose, it doesn't feel like her. It feels like a stranger.

Right now, she's sitting at the table in the kitchen, chewing the spoonful of oatmeal Rose has just fed her. She does it with lethargic movements, and she smacks loudly. That's the only sound there is. Apart from it, the house is completely quiet. Not a soothing silence, though—more like it's holding its breath as it waits for Rose to pull herself together to say the words that are so hard to get out.

She will say them today. She has promised herself.

I'll do it when she's done eating.

This is how she thinks as she takes a paper towel and wipes her mom's chin where a bit of the oatmeal has ended up. In the end, it doesn't really matter when she says it, since it falls on deaf ears. But it still doesn't feel right to do it while she's munching on her oatmeal.

Her mom isn't the only one who has disappeared into a catatonic state. Over the past few weeks, Rose has seen something similar happen to several of the neighbors in the vicinity. At first, they just acted a bit weird, like her mom did the first morning, but aside from that, they followed their usual patterns most of the time. Mr. McGee, for example, went on his walks with Frankie every day, and the couple across the street, Lilly and Dan, faithfully took their car to work every morning ... although there can't be many customers left in the clothing store they run together. There even was a day when Rose happened to be out in the driveway as they left. That day, Lilly spotted her, and they even exchanged words—the typical, trivial banter you'd expect between neighbors—albeit Lilly's voice had the characteristic drowsiness of the sick. And Rose isn't sure Lilly quite knew who she was either.

But that's how it was at first. They followed their routines. That has gradually changed. More and more often, it was Frankie the bulldog who pulled a confused Mr. McGee on the walk, and Lilly and Dan's working hours started to vary greatly.

For the past three days, Rose hasn't seen a trace of any of them, and she doesn't for a second doubt why that is. She's sure they're sitting somewhere inside their houses, staring blankly into a wall, just like her mom. Because that's how it ends.

"Just one mouthful left," she says as she scrapes the last oatmeal onto the spoon and gives it to her mom. "After that, you're all done. Was it good?"

It's weird that she keeps talking to her like that, but she can't help it. Before every meal, she always tells herself not to do it, but she still ends up talking to her as if she were a small child lost in a supermarket.

While her mom chews the last mouthful, Rose walks over to the sink and cleans the bowl. When done, she goes back to the table, helps her mom up, and leads her to the couch in the living room. There she leaves her while she herself heads upstairs for a while.

When Rose comes back down, she has her arms full

of clothes and holds a hairbrush in one hand and her mom's makeup bag in the other. The clothes consist of an emerald-green blouse with embroidery on the sleeves and a pair of jeans in a deep, indigo-blue color. It's her mom's favorite outfit.

It was her favorite outfit, she corrects herself and feels a sting of despair.

"Look," she says with forced excitement, holding up the clothes in front of her mom. "I thought we could make you extra pretty today."

Without waiting for an answer or a reaction, Rose leaves the outfit on the couch and helps her mom out of her nightgown.

"Okay, then we need to get your arms up so I can get the blouse on. Here, let me help you. That's it, good. So pretty. And now, the pants. I'm just going to grab this, and then ... voila! You'll look so nice."

When the hardest part is over—dressing her is *always* the hardest part— Rose grabs the brush and starts combing her mom's hair. She does it with slow, gentle strokes, although she probably could have torn away at it without her mom even blinking.

With similarly soft movements, she now applies a light makeup on her mom's face. She chooses a pink shade of rouge to add freshness to the cheeks which have lost most of their natural color. Above the vacant eyes, she applies a discreet layer of eye shadow, and

the lips get a neutral color, like her mom usually prefers.

While Rose works on this quiet transformation of
her mom, she also comes to terms with her own.
Because there is something symbolic about this moment. It feels important. As if she is in the process of
preparing them both for the impending farewell. For
saying goodbye to each other.

"And ... done," she says, pulling out a small mirror
from her makeup bag. "What do you think?"

Not surprisingly, Betty Lavine has the same
opinion about her makeup as she has had about everything else for the past couple of weeks. None whatso-
ever.

"I think you look great," Rose says, pulling her lips
up in a smile that will never be returned. "Hot stuff."

For a while, those words are left hanging in the
air between them as Rose studies the empty green
eyes one last time, hoping to find her mom in there
—and when she doesn't, she clears her throat and
says:

"I can't stay here any longer, Mom. There's ...
there's nothing left in Coulton. No people, no life, and
our house is ... it hurts to be here because I'm constantly reminded of Sebastian and ... and of you. Because
you're not here either, Mom. You're not."

She reaches out her hand, places it on top of her

mom's, and gives it a squeeze. It's cold and stiff. Lifeless.

"If I believed you were here, I would stay, but ... but you're not. You're gone too, and I'm alone. That's why I have to go."

Both her heart and her brain tell her it's the right thing to do. Nevertheless, saying the words fills her with shame, and she realizes that she needs to suck it up and get it over with. Otherwise, she might just end up tucking her tail between her legs and backing out. Therefore, she pushes herself up from the couch, gives her mom a kiss on the forehead, and strokes a hand over her hair.

"Bye, Mom," she whispers. "I love you."

With that, Rose turns her back on the empty shell that once housed her mom's soul and leaves the room without looking back.

Chapter Thirty

Five times in the same day. Too much to be a coincidence. Especially considering the current state of the world, where there are hardly any other vehicles on the roads. And it *is* the same dark blue van, she's sure of it. Twice she has seen it in the rearview mirror, and twice she has caught a fleeting glimpse of it between buildings because it has been driving on a road parallel to hers.

And now it's back. A small, dark blue square in the rearview mirror, far behind.

It's neither a patrol car nor a military vehicle, but even if that may appear to be a positive detail, it doesn't have to mean anything. For all she knows, the psychopathic cops may have changed strategy. Have gone undercover.

She takes her eyes off the road for a moment and glances down at the glove compartment of the car. That's where she keeps the gun that she took from Officer Mendez.

Only if absolutely necessary, she thinks, but at the same time, she knows she'll probably have a better chance if she takes the gun and confronts her pursuers head-on instead of trying to run away from them. Because while she's increased her experience as a driver by several hundred percent over the last four days, mostly spent on the road, she's still a beginner. And she remembers, far too well, what happened during her last car chase.

Four days of driving east, through city after city, hoping she would find others like her. Other normal people.

Some distance ahead, an intersection appears, and seeing it, Rose makes a choice: she is going to turn right there—and if the blue van decides to follow her, it's going to be the glove compartment.

The ensuing seconds are nerve-wracking. She sits in her seat, tightly wound, her gaze wandering back and forth between the road and the rearview mirror. She tries to keep a steady speed until she has to turn so the brake light doesn't give them a heads-up.

She reaches the intersection, turns onto the cross-road, and eases her foot slightly off the pedal, causing the car to lose speed. Then, without even realizing it, she starts counting the seconds in her head.

She gets to sixteen before she gets her answer and leans to the side to open the glove compartment.

After placing the gun in the passenger seat, Rose again puts both hands on the steering wheel and steps on the gas. She'd better use the one advantage she has got—that *she* gets to decide where the confrontation will take place. And she has already made that decision because there was a sign at the intersection that said *ONE MILE TO THE KEYSTONE CLASSIC DINER*. All things considered, it would seem more natural for her to pull in at a diner than for her to stop by the roadside out in no man's land.

Less than two minutes later, she turns into the parking lot and stops her car in front of a menu board highlighting signature dishes like the *Steel City Steak Sandwich, Farmers' Market Omelette* and *Liberty Apple Pie*. Behind the sign is the diner; a red brick building with a flat roof and large windows through which you can see the interior.

Under normal circumstances, Rose would have found the décor charming—dark wood tables and red leather chairs, surrounded by paneled walls, filled with photographs of important events and places in the state's history—but at this moment, her focus is elsewhere.

She grabs the gun from the passenger seat, gets out, and runs to the diner's entrance. She expects it to be locked, so it's a relief when she grabs it and discovers that it isn't.

The door slides open, and a small bell above her head announces her arrival to the empty room.

"Hello? Is anyone here?"

As expected, no answer—which suits her just fine.

She remains in the doorway until she hears the blue van slow down and turn into the parking lot. She doesn't dare turn around and look, but that isn't necessary either, because there is a mirror on the back wall behind the counter. Using that, she can keep an eye on the van. It's coming to a stop now, right at the parking lot's exit. For a moment, that detail has her doubting her plan. Because what if they just stay there? What will she do then?

Fortunately, that concern is quickly dismissed, because now there's a person getting out of the van and walking toward the diner. A man in a green parka coat, the hood of which hides his face.

Slowly—and with a route that keeps her visible from the outside—Rose walks up to the counter, where she disappears out of sight behind a pillar. And as soon as she's behind it, she slides to the floor and sneaks back toward the entrance, this time via a route that keeps her hidden behind chairs and tables.

When she gets to the table closest to the door, she squats, tightens her grip on the gun, and waits.

Soon the metallic jingle of the bell returns, and with it comes a cold breeze that caresses Rose's neck and sends a shiver down her spine. She closes her eyes and concentrates on listening, trying to pinpoint her pursuer's position—and once she's sure he's gotten some way into the diner, she jumps up.

"DON'T MOVE OR I'LL SHOOT!"

The man in the parka coat stiffens and quickly raises his hands.

He's not very tall. He looked much bigger when Rose saw him in the mirror earlier. However, that doesn't mean he's not dangerous.

"TURN AROUND!" she orders. "SLOWLY!"

The man does as he is told. He gradually turns around until his face appears under the hood's furry rim, and ... it's not a man? It's a woman. An old lady, actually.

"I'm sorry if I scared you," the woman says. "I didn't mean to. My name is Mary, and—"

"Are you alone?"

Behind her round glasses, the lady's brown eyes glance toward the van in the parking lot. Then she slowly shakes her head.

"No. I'm not alone. I'm with two men. Two *friendly* men. They're waiting outside in the van. We agreed that it was probably best if I was the one to approach you. I'm not so ... intimidating."

"Why are you following me? What do you want?"

The lady purses her lips in a cautious, but warm, smile.

"We want the same as you, I think. To find other people like us. Others who are still sane."

The words hit Rose hard and make her chest feel like it's shrinking. She opens her mouth but can't get any words out.

"We have been following you," the lady continues. "No point in denying that. But it was only because we wanted to make sure that you're not ill ... and that you're alone. Listen, is it okay if I put my arms down? It's hard for me to keep them up there."

Rose squints her eyes and studies the woman's hands. They look skinny and fragile. As if they're really nothing more than bones and a thin layer of wrinkled skin.

"Open your coat so I can see that you're not armed. And do it slowly."

The lady cautiously unzips the coat and opens it. To her relief, Rose sees nothing hidden inside it, and she allows herself to calm down a bit.

"Fine," she says, nodding. "You can put your hands down, but I need to be able to see them, okay?"

"Of course. Thank you. My name is Mary, by the way. I don't know if I said that already."

"You did."

"And the two out in the van are Frank and Thomas ... although no one really calls Thomas by his real name. They call him the Mayor. He's the one who started it."

"Started what?"

"Our group," Mary explains. "The Mayor was from Mellowfield, and he saved a bunch of people from the police when the Collapse had just started. After that day, they've followed him loyally. They became the first members of our flock, and since then, more have joined almost on a daily basis. Myself included."

"So ... what? You just drive around all day and pick people up or what?"

Rose is aware of the confrontational, almost juvenile tone of her voice, but she honestly has no idea how to react to what this strange lady is saying to her. Whether she is to laugh, cry, or run away screaming.

"Not quite," Mary replies calmly. "It varies who goes out to look for new members, just like most other tasks in the camp do. And actually, this is the first time I've been out. Usually, some of the younger volunteer to go so an old crow like me doesn't have to. But this time I insisted on going."

"The camp?" Rose asks. The word can barely be squeezed out of her throat.

Mary nods and smiles. The way people smile at someone with whom they share a secret.

"You're not alone," she then says. "Only if you choose to be."

Rose looks down at the gun in her hand. All of a sudden, it feels immensely heavy. Like a block of lead, increasing its weight until she finally has to give in and lower it.

"There aren't that many of us yet," Mary continues. "But I think we're about forty now, and more are coming all the time."

"Where?" Rose stammers.

"Northeast," Mary says, tilting her head slightly and glancing toward the van. "I'm really not supposed to say more than that, but we've settled in an old miners' camp, and it's a nice place to stay. It's secluded, away from the cities, and we're self-sufficient in electricity because of the mine."

Before continuing, she makes sure to catch Rose's gaze.

"Obviously, it's not perfect," she says. "But after what we've all been through, it's nice to be part of a community and have a place to belong. A home."

These are heavy words, especially the last one, and

Rose has to fight fiercely to hold back the tears in the silence that follows.

"What do you say, dear?" Mary asks. "Should I signal my companions to come in here so you can say hi to them?"

Rose looks out toward the van, then back at the lady in the green parka who has just tilted her world upside down.

Then she nods.

PART FIVE

The Boy in the Hoodie

~⚬⚬~

"Sometimes a home is somewhere.
Sometimes it's someone."

O. E. GERALT

Chapter Thirty-One

Three soft knocks on the door. Then a pause. Then two more knocks followed by Mary's melodic voice.

"Rose? Are you up?"

"Huh? Yeah, um ... I'm up."

"Are you sure?"

"Uh-huh, yeah."

That's a lie. Rose hasn't gotten up. She has barely *woken* up. But that's okay. Mary knows. It's part of their daily ritual, and Rose is pretty sure Mary enjoys waking her up as much as she enjoys staying under the blanket as long as she can get away with. It's those kinds of small, silly things that make life feel more normal after the Collapse.

Mary is her neighbor now. Like Rose, she lives in one of the many trailer homes set up in the parking lot behind the hangar-like iron building, which once served as the headquarters—and workers' residence— of the San Hiva mining company. Now its bunk beds are filled with other survivors of the end of the world. The other members of San Hiva camp.

Rose has lived in the camp for about a month, and she is beginning to think of the place as home, although admitting it to herself still evokes a sense of shame in her. But the list of things that have that effect is long, so adding one more thing won't make much difference.

She stretches, yawns loudly, and sits up in bed at exactly the moment when the next three knocks sound from the door.

"I'm up now, Mary. For real."

"That's good," is the reply. "Because I'm headed over to Joan now, and you're going on a trip today. You haven't forgotten, have you?"

"Of course not."

No, Rose hasn't forgotten what her plans for today are. How could she when she has spent so long trying to convince the Mayor to let her tag along?

Thomas Longhorn, that's his real name, is a good leader and a good person ... but he can also be stubborn as a mule. And since he had gotten it into his head that Rose was too young to go out to search for survivors, she had to harass him on a daily basis for almost an entire week before he caved and gave her permission. On the condition that he also took part in the trip, of course. But that's okay. She would rather go with the Mayor than with the new guy they brought in a few days ago. Jack something. He gave the impression of being a bit of a troublemaker.

After wriggling out of her worn sleeping bag, Rose gets up and walks barefoot across the icy metal floor to the chair in the corner where she stores her clothes. Once dressed, she prepares her breakfast—two fried eggs and a piece of toast—and eats it. Finally, she brushes her hair and teeth, after which she opens the door of the trailer and steps outside.

It's a cold but beautiful day. The rays of the morning sun glimmer on the metal plates of the trailers, and the temperature is low enough to turn her breath into small, white clouds.

It's a strange sight. She thinks that every morning, and this one is no exception. The camp is an attempt to restore some semblance of normality, while at the same time, it's such a clear symbol of the civilized world having collapsed. Nothing shows it better than the difference between Mary's trailer home and the next, which belongs to a man named Mitchell. Both homes have a small, fenced area at the front, and Mary has chosen to fill hers with flowers in pots as if it were a tiny garden, while Mitchell's is filled with a chaotic jumble of old car tires and wooden pallets.

Order set against chaos. Hope against resignation. The question remains whose world it is they're actually living in now.

With that thought in her head, Rose takes one last look at her own little base before heading over to the other side of the paved parking lot, where the Mayor has set up his home in an old Winnebago RV.

Once there, she stops and takes a moment to read the sign next to the door. It must be one he has just put up, because she can't recall having seen it before. And with that text—*YES, YES, THE WORLD HAS ENDED, BUT YOU CAN STILL KNOCK FIRST!*—she reckons that she would have remembered it.

She follows the unambiguous instructions and knocks on the door.

"Come on in," says a male voice on the other side, but before Rose reaches the handle, he has already opened the door from the inside. Now he stands in front of her, the good Mayor; a short, broad-shouldered man with coarse facial features and a scalp that, except for a single cluster of cork-brown hair, is completely bare.

"Good morning, Mr. Longhorn."

"Good morning, Rose. I'm almost ready. I just need to talk to Marlon about the incident with the generator at the radio house. It'll only take a few minutes. You can study the route in the meantime. I've put the map there on the table."

"Okay. We decided on Newcrest, right?"

"Yeah. We've been there once before, but it's a big city, so there can easily be more."

"I'll take a look at it."

The Mayor gives her a raised thumb, then zips up his jacket and rushes out the door. As soon as he's gone, Rose sits down and looks at the map, which lies on a small, fold-out desk in the center section of the RV.

When the Mayor returns—ten minutes later, not two—he is not alone. He's been joined by Hank Thimble, about whom Rose knows little more than that he's the camp's expert when it comes to vehicle repair and maintenance. Whether he was actually a mechanic before the Collapse, she doesn't know, since she hasn't exchanged much more than a few courtesy phrases with him. He does fit her image of a mechanic, though. He almost always has smudges of oil on his hands and his cheeks, and no matter what clothes he wears, there's always a wrench sticking out from one of the pockets.

"Hank is joining us today," the Mayor says.

Rose nods, first to him, then to Hank, after which she gets up, folds the map, and hands it to the Mayor ...

who stares at it as if it was a steaming hot pile of dog poo she was trying to give him.

"And what am I supposed to do with that?" he says dryly. "You're the one who studied the route, right?"

Rose opens her mouth, hesitates, and closes it again. Then she nods.

"Then it's settled," the Mayor concludes. "What do you say we get moving then?"

Without waiting for an answer, he turns around and walks out the door. And after exchanging a confused look, Rose and Hank do the same.

Chapter Thirty-Two

The hanged people in the crossbeams of the Haywood Bridge aren't the first they've seen on the trip. Far from it. But there's something particularly menacing about these three.

Part of it is the way they are hanging. The structure of it. As if the perpetrator has really thought about making it symmetrical so that they form a V whose acute angle points toward the center of the bridge, almost like an arrow. Another part is the way the wind makes them sway slightly from side to side in time, making it appear as if they are consciously following each other's movements.

On the other side of the bridge awaits Newcrest—a medium-sized city, now devoid of life, so the sky-scrapers in its skyline seem more like the giant tombstones of an oversized cemetery than proud symbols of achievement.

From her place in the passenger seat, Rose silently watches the desolate streets glide by as they drive toward the center of the city. Sidewalks that no one strolls on anymore and store windows that nobody glances through any longer.

"First time here?" the Mayor asks from the driver's seat.

Rose replies with a nod but doesn't move her gaze from the window.

"It's a damned sad sight," Hank interjects from the back seat. "It used to be such a vibrant city, so full of life."

"The world used to be full of life," the Mayor adds dryly, after which he nods toward the map on Rose's lap. "Are we on the right track?"

"We have to turn right in a minute. Not at the next intersection, but the one that comes after it."

She lifts her finger to point but stops halfway through the movement when something in the side mirror catches her attention. A vehicle crossing the road some distance behind.

She turns around in her seat and squints her eyes, only to catch one more fleeting glimpse of the car before it has completely disappeared out of sight.

"What's the matter?"

"A car."

"A car? Where?"

"At the intersection we went through just before. There was a car that crossed it."

"What kind?" Hank says, and Rose is about to ask why that matters when she realizes what he's really asking.

"Not a police car," she says. "It was brown. A station wagon, I think."

She looks at their driver, asking him without words what the next step is. He responds by pressing the brake and making a U-turn. Then he speeds up.

When they've reached the intersection, the Mayor turns sharply left and continues onto the adjacent road ... but there are no longer any traces of the brown station wagon. It's just another empty street with abandoned shops on one side and a deserted city park on the other. From one of the park's trees hangs a woman who—as an ironic comment on their situation —is dressed in a blouse with a large, bronze-colored question mark printed on the front.

"What do you say, chief?" Hank asks from the back seat. "Do we go back, or—"

"We keep going," the Mayor replies promptly. "It can't have gone far."

But it could have turned onto a side street, Rose thinks.

However, she chooses to keep that observation to herself.

For the next while, the Mayor keeps driving straight ahead on the same road, while Rose scans the cityscape outside, hoping that she will spot the brown station wagon. As the minutes pass, however, she gradually loses faith that she will. In fact, she's on the verge of throwing in the towel when the large building with the three giant letters on the facade appears.

N.M.H. it says—and underneath, in a smaller font: *Newcrest Memorial Hospital.*

Below the sign is the entrance of the hospital, and a bit to the left of that is the brown station wagon.

Rose places her hand on the Mayor's forearm to get his attention. Once she has it, she points toward the hospital.

"Well, I'll be damned," he whispers, after which he slows down and lets the car roll until it stops on its own.

"What are they doing?" Hank asks. "Is that ... a car?"

He doesn't elaborate further, but there is no need for that either. Rose is well aware of what he's referring to. And yes, to her it also looks like a car—or rather a car *wreck*, given that it has been flipped upside down and looks as if it has been on fire. It's jammed between the two walls on both sides of the hospital entrance. Where the doors should have been.

At the rear of the burned car, a man is kneeling. It looks like he's trying to open the trunk. Some distance to his left stands another person. He has his back turned and is wearing a hoodie, the hood of which is pulled up so Rose can't make out a lot of details about him. Still, there's something—perhaps his posture—that gives her the impression that he's younger than his partner.

"I think he got it open now," Hank says.

Rose lets her gaze drift back to the man at the rear of the burned car. Sure enough, he has gotten the trunk open and taken something out of it. It's blue. Looks kind of like a plastic folder, similar to the ones Rose used for her school papers.

Now the man stands up and inspects his discovery —and while he studies the contents of the folder, Rose studies him. He seems to be somewhere in the middle, perhaps the end, of his forties and a fan of heavy metal judging by his attire and his long silver-gray hair secured in a ponytail.

With the folder in hand, the man now strolls over to his partner to exchange a few words before they both walk back to the brown station wagon and get in.

"Do we drive over there?"

The Mayor ponders for a moment and then shakes his head.

"Let's keep an eye on them first. From a distance. See what they're up to."

After those words, he turns off the headlights. Then he locks his gaze on the brown station wagon and waits. So do his two fellow travelers.

For a while, nothing happens. The station wagon just stays in the hospital's empty parking lot—for so long that Rose starts to think that they may have been spotted. That the two strangers could be devising a strategy to escape.

But then the rear light suddenly flashes red, and the car starts to drive out of the parking lot. And it doesn't look like they're in a hurry to get away.

The Mayor waits patiently until they're all the way out on the road. Then he follows.

Chapter Thirty-Three

The realization hits Rose and the Mayor at exactly the same second. They've been outsmarted. They've followed the brown station wagon from a distance all the way back through the deserted streets of Newcrest, and there hasn't been the slightest sign that they've been discovered.

Until now, when the trap has sprung. A trap that they've walked right into.

They're back on the same bridge that they crossed when they drove into town—and they got almost twenty-five yards onto it before realizing that the brown station wagon had stopped at the end. And those twenty-five yards mean that they are currently next to the guardrail that separates the bridge's two lanes—making them so narrow that a U-turn is impossible.

"Can you back out?"

The Mayor shakes his head and lifts his index finger from the steering wheel so it points out through the windshield. Rose looks—and gets her answer.

The two people they've been following have gotten out of the station wagon. They are leaning against its rear, and one of them—the man with the long silvery hair—holds a rifle in his hands. He doesn't aim it at them, but he would have ample time to do so should they decide to back away. And they would be an easy target, stuck in the narrow lane.

The Mayor exchanges a glance with Rose and Hank, and after receiving a nod from both of them, he takes a deep breath and lets the air out in a lengthy sigh. Then he puts the car in gear and drives forward.

As he stops the car again, about fifty feet from them, the two strangers start moving toward them. They walk without haste, and the gun still isn't aimed at them, which must be a good sign.

Another good sign is their faces. They look vigilant but not hostile. Especially the young man with the hoodie, whom Rose can now see properly for the first time. He has blond hair, a disheveled mane that drapes down over his forehead, almost covering his eyes.

He is young. About her own age, maybe even a little younger.

Now the man with the ponytail stops next to the window in the driver's side and makes a circular motion in the air with one hand.

The Mayor nods and rolls down the window, doing his best to smile disarmingly.

"Good afternoon," the man in the ponytail says in a voice that perfectly matches his appearance; worn and a bit rusty. "We thought that we might as well stop and ask why you're following us."

"I assure you that we mean no harm," the Mayor says, holding his hands up in front of him as if that somehow proves the claim. "My name is Thomas Longhorn. My companions and me are members of a larger group made up of survivors of ... well, we've dubbed it *The Collapse*, but what we call it doesn't really matter."

"The Collapse?" the man with the ponytail repeats. "Oh, well, why not? Listen, Thomas Longhorn, why don't you and your friends come out here? I'm a much better listener if I can see your hands."

The Mayor glances at Rose, who nods. Behind her, Hank does the same.

"Yes, of course. We're coming out now."

With those words, he opens the door and steps out. Rose reaches for the door handle on her side, but the

young man in the hoodie beats her to it. He opens the
door for her and then takes a step backward to give her
space. Part of her finds this gesture somewhat absurd,
given the situation. Another part of her finds it quite
charming.

"Much better," says Mr. Ponytail over on the other
side of the car. "But I think I interrupted you. You were
about to tell us how incredibly peaceful you are,
weren't you?"

The Mayor purses his lips in a smile, although Rose
isn't sure he found the comment particularly funny.

"As I said, we come from a larger group," he says.
"We have a camp. A safe and stable place that we are
trying to transform into a small community."

"A camp? Where?"

"East."

"Fair enough."

"As far as resources go, we're doing quite well," the
Mayor continues. "We have water, we have food, and
we have bunk beds in abundance. We're even self-
sufficient in electricity."

"Why do I get the feeling there's a *but* coming?"

"*But* a strong community requires people. The
more, the better. For that reason, we have been looking
for other survivors, right from the start. Survivors who
would like to become part of a larger community."

As the Mayor says the last words, Rose notices a change in the face of the young man in the hoodie. It's gone again almost immediately, but she catches it, and she knows exactly what it is. Because she has felt the same loneliness and the same longing, and she clearly remembers how she felt when Mary told her about the camp.

Now he discovers that she is staring at him, and her gaze falls to the ground in embarrassment. But when she dares to look up again, she finds him smiling at her.

"That's all very well and good," says the man with the ponytail. "But we've already got a home."

"And of course, we respect that," the Mayor hastens to say. "But perhaps we can still help each other out."

"I'm gonna need you to specify that, I think."

"Certainly. Hank, would you mind showing these gentlemen what we have in the trunk?"

Hank nods and starts to turn around but is immediately stopped by the man in the ponytail.

"Not him," he says, after which he nods toward Rose. "The girl."

"As you wish. Rose, could you?"

Rose nods and then looks questioningly at the man in the ponytail. He gives his permission with a small nod before turning to his partner.

"You go with her, David. I'll keep an eye on these two in the meantime."

Rose waits until the young man is at her side, and then they walk together to the trunk of the car.

"Is your friend always that distrusting?" she whispers as she pulls the handle and opens the tailgate.

For a split second, the young man looks serious, almost offended, and Rose wishes she could take back the words ... but then he curls his lips up in a smile.

"Tommy is actually a really nice guy," he says. "We're just not used to meeting ... people like you out here, that's all."

"Normal people, you mean?"

He nods and then shifts his gaze down to the trunk as if to signal that they'd better get back to work.

"It's this one he wants to show you," Rose says, pointing to a cardboard box in the left side. She pulls it into the center of the trunk and opens it. Under the flaps is a carefully selected assortment of items that any given survivor should be able to see the value of. Cans of food and a small box with medicine and basic first aid equipment.

"It's for you," she says, smiling. "Can I bring it around so your buddy can see it too?"

The young man in the hoodie responds by making a *go ahead* motion with his hand. Rose lifts the cardboard box out of the trunk, carries it around the car, and puts it on the ground in front of the man with the ponytail.

He studies it for a moment and then pushes one of the flaps open with the tip of his shoe.

"We get that you're wary of strangers," the Mayor says. "Frankly, it would be more worrying if you weren't. But to show our goodwill, we always bring a box like that one. It's for you—and we ask for nothing more than that you will think about what we've told you. Because as I said, I do believe we can help each other out ... also without us having to live in the same place. There are still plenty of benefits to knowing someone who may have access to resources and knowledge that you don't have yourself. So, take whatever time you need, talk it through—and if you decide to give us a chance, there's a note at the bottom of the box with a radio frequency that you can contact us on. We keep our radio open every afternoon from five to seven."

For a long time, the man with the ponytail stares at the box without saying anything. Then he scratches his cheek and makes eye contact with his young companion. And only after the two of them have exchanged a nod does he shift his attention back to the Mayor.

"Tommy Morgan," he says, holding out his hand.

The Mayor shakes it—and while he does that, the

young man in the hoodie reaches his hand out toward Rose.

"David," he says as she accepts it. "And your name is Rose, right?"

"Nice to meet you, David ... and yeah, my name is Rose."

As the man in the ponytail moves on to Hank to shake his hand, the Mayor walks over and greets David. He then turns to Rose, placing a hand on her elbow.

"Will you help the young man put the box in their car? It's getting cold out here, and there's no reason for us to keep them from moving on."

Rose nods and then walks over to pick up the cardboard box, but once again David beats her to it.

"I've got it," he says, picking up the box. "You can get the trunk for me. It's not locked."

Once David has loaded the box into the trunk, Rose closes the hatch and starts walking back. However, after only taking a few steps, she hesitates and looks at him instead.

"Hey, can I ask you something?"

"Uh, yeah, of course."

"That wrecked car at the hospital ... was that yours? And what was that thing you took from it?"

David looks at her, a cautious smile forming on his lips.

"It's a long story," he says. "But, um … if you'd like to hear it, then maybe I can tell you over the radio someday?"

Rose thinks about it for a moment. Then she returns his smile and nods.

"I think I'd like that."

Afterword

It's not without ambivalence that I sit here now, staring at the final page of the story. Because it's no secret that I had fun writing the original *Strung* trilogy, and it has been a true pleasure for me to return to that world for a while.

As mentioned in the dedication, I wrote *Rose's Story* for the fans of the *Strung* books, and I hope it lives up to their expectations. I know I've tried my best to hit the style and pacing of the original trilogy. I also hope that readers feel they have gotten an extra perspective on both the world of the books and Rose as a character.

Another thing that made this story extra fun to write was that I got to kill one of my readers. Before I started writing *Rose's Story*, we ran a competition through the editorial, letting the winner become a character in the book. So, the unfortunate teacher who is executed by the two officers is actually a real person. Her name is Kristal Shanahan, she *is* a teacher, though not in Pennsylvania, and she has been really nice and obliging during the process. So, thank you for that, Kristal. And yes, I had warned her that she probably wouldn't make it to the last page—and she was fine with it.

I guess, on the whole, it must really seem like I just love killing my characters. Especially in this story, where almost the entire cast is sent out on the plank and pushed down to the sharks—or in this case, the murderous police officers. As for that, I really didn't have much choice this time around. For as the observant reader of *Strung 2* will recall, it says that Randall regarded Rose's story as one of the worst examples of how the psychopathic police force had made the first fortnight after the invasion a living hell for the survivors. That it had been an outright massacre and that within days she lost her entire network of friends and family. So, that's what I had to work with. A corner I had painted myself into, you might say.

But that's okay, because a good portion of her story was already in the back of my mind at the time, and in many respects, it also guided her behavior in *Strung 2*. For instance, Rose's relationship with Billy has always been colored by the way she lost her mother. She takes care of Billy and is compensated with bright moments, which she never got with her mother. The negative consequence, of course, is that it also made her blind to what Billy really was—and we all know what that cost her during the Redwater massacre.

So, is this the end of *Strung* books? For now, yes. There's still one story in the universe that keeps popping up in the back of my mind, but it only comes to me in small fragments, and I don't know if it will end up making a full image. It's the story of the first officer to change. Patient zero, if you like. I think his story could be interesting—especially because I have this feeling that he's a really nice guy.

But yeah, for now, this is where the ride ends—and if you've been with me all the way, I hope you've enjoyed it as much as I have.

—PER JACOBSEN

Thanks to ...

Sarah Jacobsen, my boo, my bae, my old ball-and-chain. My missus, my queen, and my pure royal pain. My mamacita, my anchor, my partner in crime. My boss lady, main lady, homegirl, and tight-wound life-line. My here for the sad and here for the fun. My better half, my constant +1.

Kaare & Karina Bertelsen Dantoft, my ass-kicking beta reader team.

Last but never least, as always, I owe a huge thanks to you, **dear reader**. Time is precious and I thank you from the bottom of my heart for yours.

—PER JACOBSEN